The

BEST
BAD
LUCK

I Ever Had

The BEST BAD LUCK I Ever Had

Kristin Levine

G. P. Putnam's Sons

G. P. PUTNAM'S SONS
A division of Penguin Young Readers Group.
Published by The Penguin Group.
Penguin Group (USA) Inc., 375 Hudson Street, New York, NY 10014, U.S.A.
Penguin Group (Canada), 90 Eglinton Avenue East, Suite 700, Toronto, Ontario M4P 2Y3, Canada
(a division of Pearson Penguin Canada Inc.).
Penguin Books Ltd, 80 Strand, London WC2R 0RL, England.
Penguin Ireland, 25 St. Stephen's Green, Dublin 2, Ireland (a division of Penguin Books Ltd.).
Penguin Group (Australia), 250 Camberwell Road, Camberwell, Victoria 3124, Australia
(a division of Pearson Australia Group Pty Ltd).
Penguin Books India Pvt Ltd, 11 Community Centre, Panchsheel Park, New Delhi—110 017, India.
Penguin Group (NZ), 67 Apollo Drive, Rosedale, North Shore 0632, New Zealand
(a division of Pearson New Zealand Ltd).
Penguin Books (South Africa) (Pty) Ltd, 24 Sturdee Avenue, Rosebank,
Johannesburg 2196, South Africa.
Penguin Books Ltd, Registered Offices: 80 Strand, London WC2R 0RL, England.

Library of Congress Cataloging-in-Publication Data
Levine, Kristin (Kristin Sims), 1974–
The best bad luck I ever had / Kristin Levine.
p.   cm.
Summary: In Moundville, Alabama, in 1917, twelve-year-old Dit hopes the new postmaster
will have a son his age, but instead he meets Emma, who is black, and their friendship
challenges accepted ways of thinking and leads them to save the life of a condemned man.
[1. Race relations—Fiction.   2. Prejudices—Fiction.   3. Friendship—Fiction.
4. Country life—Alabama—Fiction.   5. Family life—Alabama—Fiction.
6. Alabama—History—1819–1950—Fiction.]   I. Title.
PZ7.L57842Bes 2009   [Fic]—dc22   2008011570

ISBN 978-0-399-25090-3
1   3   5   7   9   10   8   6   4   2

To my grandfather,
the real Harry Otis

1

THE NEW POSTMASTER

I'VE BEEN WRONG BEFORE. OH, HECK, IF I'M being real honest, I've been wrong a lot. But I ain't never been so wrong as I was about Emma Walker. When she first came to town, I thought she was the worst piece of bad luck I'd had since falling in the outhouse on my birthday. I tell you, things were fine in Moundville before Emma got here, least I thought they were. Guess the truth is, you'll never know how wrong I was till I'm done telling and explaining—so I'd better just get on with the story.

My real name is Harry Otis Sims, but everybody calls me Dit. See, when I was little, I used to roll a hoop down Main Street, beating it with a stick as I ran along. One day, two older boys tried to steal my hoop. I hit them with my stick and told them, "Dit away." They laughed. "You talk like a baby. Dit, dit, dit." The name stuck.

There are ten children in our family: Della, Ollie, Ulman, Elman, Raymond, me, Earl, Pearl, Robert and Lois. That's just too many kids. There are never leftovers at supper, and you never get new clothes. We don't even get to go to the store for shoes: Mama just keeps them all in a big old barrel. When the pair you're wearing gets too tight, you throw yours in and pick out another one. With so many kids, sometimes I think my pa don't even know my name, since it's always, "Della, Ollie, Ulman, Elman, Raymond, uh, I mean Dit."

We all live in a big old house that Pa built himself right off Main Street in Moundville, Alabama. Most of the people in Moundville are farmers like my pa. Just about everything grows well in our rich, dark soil, but especially corn and cotton. Before I even had my nickname, Pa taught me how to count by showing me the number of ears of corn to feed the mule.

Most evenings my whole family, and just about everybody in town, gathers in front of Mrs. Pooley's General Goods Store to wait for the train. Mrs. Pooley is the meanest old lady I've ever met. She smokes, spits and has a temper shorter than a bulldog's tail. But her store has a wide, comfortable porch and a great view of the train depot, just across the street. The evening Emma came, Mrs. Pooley sat in her usual rocker, smoking a pipe with Uncle Wiggens.

Uncle Wiggens ain't really my uncle, everyone just calls him that. He's over eighty and fought in the War Between the States. He only has one leg and one hero, General Robert E. Lee. Uncle Wiggens manages to work Lee's name into pretty much any old conversation. You might say, "My, it's cold today," and he'd reply, "You think this is cold? General Lee said it didn't even qualify as chill till your breath froze on your nose and made a little icicle." He had about five different stories of how he lost his leg, every one of them entertaining.

That night I was listening to the version that involved him running five Yankees into a bear's den as I wound a ball of twine into a baseball. Course if I'd had the money, I could have bought a new ball at Mrs. Pooley's store, but if you wind twine real careful, it's almost as good as a real ball.

The new postmaster was coming to town, and the grown-ups were as wound up as the kids on Christmas. The postmaster was in charge of sorting and delivering the mail, but he also sent and received telegrams. This meant he knew any good gossip long before anybody else. The last postmaster had been a lazy good-for-nothing: everyone had gotten the wrong mail two days late. He and his family had finally skipped town for refusing to pay their debts at Mrs. Pooley's store.

I was excited too. The new postmaster, Mr. Walker, was supposed to have a boy who was twelve, just like me. I sure hoped he liked to play baseball. It was June 1917, and my best friend, Chip, had just left to spend the summer with his grandma in Selma.

My ball of twine got bigger and bigger till there was a small light, far off in the distance. We all jumped up and ran across the street to the train depot. There was a flash of copper as the golden eagle on the top of the huge locomotive flew out of the night sky. The whistle howled, white steam poured out of the engine and the train came to a slow stop in front of the station.

A few local men who worked in Tuscaloosa got off first. Next, a couple of townspeople who had been visiting relatives climbed down the steps. Finally, a thin girl nobody knew appeared in the doorway of the train.

The girl looked about my age and wore a fancy navy dress. Her hair was carefully combed and pulled back into a neat braid, tied with a red ribbon. She clutched a small suitcase of smooth leather. She was also colored.

2

THE GIRL FROM BOSTON

THE GIRL STOOD IN THE DOORWAY OF THE train as the whole town looked her over. My little sister Pearl stared at her shoes—shiny, black patent leather without a scuff on them. Pearl's ten years old and ain't never had a pair that ain't been worn by two sisters before her. The girl's mother stepped into the doorway right behind her. She was colored too and wore a yellow dress made of a gauzy material—Mama later said it was organza.

The girl and her mama stepped carefully down onto the platform. Her daddy got off last. He wore a tailored suit, walked with a limp and was just as black as the rest of them.

The man looked around and in a crisp, Northern accent asked, "Is there a Mr. Sims here?"

"I'm Mr. Sims," said Pa, looking a bit confused.

"I'm Mr. Walker," said the man, holding out his hand. "The new postmaster."

It got real quiet for a moment. Everyone stared at Mr. Walker.

"They is niggers," said Uncle Wiggens, just as loud as could be.

Pa stepped forward then and shook Mr. Walker's hand.

"The boy's a girl," I mumbled. Mama poked me with her elbow, then went to speak to Mrs. Walker.

I scowled at the girl. "What's your name?"

"Emma," she said, and scowled right back.

Mama made me carry home Emma's trunk in my old wagon. We had a cabin on our property that we always rented out to the postmaster and his family. I didn't understand how one little girl could have more stuff than me and all my brothers.

"You play baseball?" I asked as we walked.

"No," Emma said. She shook her feet as she walked, trying to keep the dust off her fancy shoes.

"I got a real glove." I tugged at the wagon. "The only one in town."

"Maybe down south girls play baseball," she answered, "but we're from Boston."

I didn't say nothing.

She pulled at the ribbon in her hair. "You probably don't even know where that is."

"Kentucky," I answered. "I ain't stupid."

Emma slowed down to walk beside her mama. "Mama," Emma said, loud enough for me to hear. "Why'd we have to come down south?"

"Emma," Mrs. Walker said softly. "I've already told you. Daddy can't protest where they send him. There aren't many Negroes in the postal service."

Emma glanced at me, then back at her mama. "I don't think I'm going to like it here."

"It's only for a year," Mrs. Walker continued. "Then Daddy can ask for a transfer."

A whole year, I thought. That was a long time to wait for another postmaster. But maybe then we'd finally get a boy.

Next morning at breakfast, I sat down next to Ulman. He's four years older than me and real smart. I leaned over to him and asked, "Boston's in Kentucky, ain't it?"

"No," he said. "It's in Massachusetts."

"Oh," I answered. I was suddenly mighty interested in my scrambled eggs.

3

DOING THE WASH

AFTER BREAKFAST, I DID MY CHORES. ALL of us kids have jobs 'cept little Robert and Lois, who are only four and two. Mine are to bring coal into the house, chop wood, drive the cows to pasture in the morning and bring them home in the evening. We always have at least three cows so we'll have enough milk and butter. Our main pasture is across the railroad tracks, and those stupid cows always stop right over the iron rails. I have to beat the cows with a switch to get them to move on. Raymond is our main milker. He's fourteen, and everybody says I look just like him 'cept my hair is red and his is brown. He's a bit taller and his nose is bigger and I'm much better looking, but other than that, we could be twins.

The morning after Emma came, I had finished my chores and was getting ready to go off hunting when Mama asked me to come help with the washing. Course it wasn't a request, it was an order, but grown-ups like to pretend they are being all reasonable even when they ain't. Washing was usually Della and Ollie's job. They're nineteen and seventeen and just about all grown up. Mama said they were both in bed 'cause their friend had come to visit. Now, I don't get to stay in bed when my friends come over, but when I told Mama that, she told me to stop being fresh and go outside.

Ten-year-old Earl and Pearl had been drafted into helping too. They really are twins, but are as alike as a chicken and a chipmunk. Earl's the chipmunk, quiet and watching everything, while Pearl's the one poking her beak into everybody's business. I felt a little better when I saw them helping because I hate doing the washing. Stirring that stupid old pot till your hands go numb. Rubbing all the water out on the wringer till your fingers are as wrinkled as the wet sheets. It's almost as bad as churning butter, and even Mama agrees that is the worst chore of all.

The wash pot is huge, and we have to pull up every bucket of water from our well. Pearl was pulling as fast as she could, but it would take forever if I let her do it. I grabbed the rope and began to yank it like the halter of a stubborn mule. The bucket came up over the lip of the well and sloshed a mouthful of water all over Pearl. I laughed as she wiped at her face with her skirt.

Earl was trying to keep the huge fire going under the big black pot. It took a lot of heat to boil all that water. It seemed like I had pulled up about a hundred buckets (and spilled two more of them on Pearl) by the time Mama came out of the house. She was balancing a huge load of sheets on her hip. Even after ten kids, Mama's long hair was still brown—mostly— and though her hands were wrinkled, her eyes were sharp. I thought she was real pretty, even if she wasn't skinny like Mrs. Walker.

While we were working, Emma was sitting on her front

porch, lazing about. This irked me no end. So I came up with a plan. "Traveling, you sure do get dusty," I said in a loud voice.

Mama ignored me.

"Remember how you used to share the washing with the last postmaster's wife? Be nice to do that again." I admit, I was sassing her a little. But I didn't care who helped, long as it wasn't me. "Bet the new neighbors have a whole mess of clothes to wash."

Mama glared at me and threw the sheets into the pot. Earl stirred them with an old broom handle. Pearl whispered, "They is Negras, Dit."

Mama glanced over at the cabin. Emma sat in her rocking chair, watching us.

"Your mama home?" Mama called over to Emma.

"Yes." Emma glided back and forth in her chair like she was bored.

"Tell her I'd like to speak to her."

Took Emma a minute to get up, as if she was thinking of disobeying Mama, but finally she disappeared into the house. Pearl's eyes got as big as a hoot owl's. "Our clothes are gonna end up all black and dirty," she said.

"Hush, child," said Mama.

Mrs. Walker came out of the house, drying her hands on a white starched apron. "Did you want something, Mrs. Sims?"

Mama rubbed her hands on the front of her own dirty dress. Earl forgot to stir. Mama said, "I was wondering, Mrs. Walker, if you wanted to do some laundry."

"Excuse me?" Mrs. Walker arched her eyebrows.

"Thursday's wash day around here," Mama explained.

"Mrs. Sims, I am not your maid."

"What?" asked Mama.

"Just because we're renting this house from you does not mean you can order me around." Mrs. Walker sounded like she was talking to a small child.

Mama rubbed a soapy hand across her forehead. "But . . ."

"Why's this so hard for you to understand? I'm not doing your wash!"

I started to laugh. "My mama ain't asking you to do the washing," I said.

Mama turned as red as one of the tomatoes in the garden. "Hush, Dit! If Mrs. Walker don't want to wash her clothes with ours, that's fine. Just more work for her."

Mama walked back toward the pot, grabbed the broom handle from Earl and began stirring furiously.

Emma took a step forward. "You mean, you wanted to do it together?" she asked.

"That's what I said, ain't it?" Mama answered. She continued to stir.

Mrs. Walker pursed her lips. "Our clothes are rather dusty from the trip," she admitted.

Mama gave a weak smile. "Dit, you can go now."

I grinned. My plan had worked.

"But why don't you show Emma around while me and Mrs. Walker wash the clothes."

Not quite as I had expected. "But Pearl . . ."

"Pearl's got to change her clothes," Mama said without looking at me. "Someone got her all wet filling the laundry tub."

Now Mama looked at me, and I knew I was stuck with Emma.

Emma didn't seem too pleased either. She folded her arms across her chest. "I didn't play with white boys in Boston."

"Well, darling," Mama said, "things is a little bit different down here."

4

THE MOUNDS

WHEN MAMA TOLD ME TO GO PLAY WITH
Emma, I decided to take her to the top of my favorite mound.
See, Moundville gets its name from the huge mounds of dirt
that are spread out among the trees, twenty-six mounds in all.
Pa says they were built by Indians carrying baskets of dirt and
dumping them out, one on top of the other. Some of our
mounds are over sixty feet high, so that's a lot of dirt.

Don't know why the Indians built them mounds. Ulman
said something about a temple for heathen gods; Elman claimed
they needed a lookout. But if you ask me, I say it was a scheme
come up with by some old woman to punish naughty children.
Ain't nothing worse than hauling dirt.

Only took a couple of minutes for me to lead Emma through
a field and a bit of wood to my mound. This was the place I
went when I wanted to be alone. It wasn't the tallest mound,
but it had the best view when you climbed to the top. The
mound was steep and covered with pricker bushes too, which
made it a hard climb. I figured Emma wouldn't like getting
sweaty and dirty and that climbing the mound would be the
best way to get rid of her.

Sure enough, Emma took one look up the steep grassy hill and shook her head. "No thank you," she said.

"No thank you, what?" I said, playing dumb.

"I'm not really that interested in climbing your mound after all. Please take me home."

"I'm going up," I said, "but you're free to go back on your own."

Emma turned on her heel and marched back toward the woods. When she reached the edge, she paused and glanced at me again. "I'm not sure I know the way."

"Then I guess you'd better come with me."

Emma took one last longing look at the woods, then trudged back over to where I was standing.

"Okay, then," I said. "Now as you may see, this mound is kind of steep. So what you need to do is hold on to the base of these shrubs and use them to pull yourself up."

I demonstrated, scrambling a few feet up the mound.

Emma grabbed a couple of leaves and pulled. The branch she was clutching broke off and she tumbled to the ground.

"The base," I said. "You grab the leaves, they'll fall right off."

Emma nodded and tried again. This time she got a pricker bush. She screamed and let go, falling down in the dirt again.

I shook my head.

Tears formed in her eyes as she held her hand up as if it were broken. "I don't think I can do this."

"Shoot, you haven't even given it a try." This girl was more a baby than I expected. "But if you're gonna cry about it, forget it. You can wait here and I'll pick you up on my way home."

"No," said Emma. She stuck her finger in her mouth and pulled out the thorn with her teeth. "I'm not a crybaby."

I started on up the hill, and Emma followed as best she could. By the time we got to the top, Emma only had a couple more scratches on her hands, but she was complaining like she was taking a bath with bees.

"If this is what you do for fun around here," Emma said as she tried to brush a smudge of dirt off her dress, "I'm never going to leave my front porch."

Fine with me, I thought. But all I said was, "Quit your whining," and led Emma to the edge of the mound to see the view.

The tops of the trees were as bushy and soft as green-dyed cotton. The Black Warrior River wound lazily through the forest. The fields of corn spread out in shades of brown and beige. Between the fields, a train chugged along, tooting its horn and letting off a stream of smoke. The sun shone down through hazy clouds and caused everything to shimmer.

"Wow," Emma breathed.

I knew what she meant. I'd seen this view a thousand times, but it still made me feel big and small at the same time.

Emma shook her head. Her mama had plaited her hair into little braids and tied the ends with bits of ribbon. "I take it back," Emma said. "This view is worth the scolding I'm going to get when my mama sees my dress."

I frowned. She wasn't supposed to like it that much. This was my place, and I didn't need no company. "Want to see something else?" I asked.

"Sure."

I took my flip-it out of my back pocket. This was a slingshot I had made by whittling down an old stick till it had two strong prongs and a comfortable handle. This particular one I had made out of a piece of driftwood from the Black Warrior. I cut a strip of rubber from an old automobile tire and a little piece of leather from the tongue of an old shoe and tied them together. With my flip-it, I could hit just about anything.

"Find me a little stone," I said to Emma.

She picked one up and handed it to me. "See that bird?" I said, pointing to a yellowhammer picking ants off a nearby tree. The yellowhammer is actually a kind of woodpecker, with bright yellow feathers under its wings that are only visible when it flies. They are as common as ants in Moundville.

"Yes," Emma answered.

I put the rock in my flip-it and let it fly. The bird was stretching out its neck for another ant. When the rock hit it, the yellowhammer fell to the ground.

"You killed it!" Emma gasped.

"Yeah," I said, grinning. Everyone was always real impressed with my flip-it skills.

Emma looked at me like I was a pig with slop all over its face. Then she turned and ran toward the fallen bird. I caught a glimpse of its yellow feathers as she picked it up.

"Want to see me get another?" I called out.

Emma didn't answer. She had a stick in one hand and was trying to dig a hole in the ground.

"What you doing?" I asked.

"You killed it," she repeated.

"You bury it in the ground, it's just gonna rot."

"What do you want to do with it?" The frown on her face let me know she was definitely not a pig lover.

"I'm gonna feed it to the eagle."

Emma put her hands on her hips. "I don't see an eagle."

So I wrapped up the bird in a large leaf, tucked it in my pocket and led Emma down the mound to Big Foot's house.

Big Foot was the town sheriff, a large man, tall as one of our mounds and mean as a hooked snapper. He lived in a small wooden house given to him by his mama, Mrs. Pooley, who owned the general store. The house had been well built once, but now it needed a new paint job and the front porch was beginning to sag. In one corner of the yard was a large iron cage, where an old eagle slept with her head tucked under her wing. I rapped on the bars to wake the bird up, then threw the dead yellowhammer into the cage. The leaf wrapper fell away. The eagle lifted her head and devoured the dead bird in a few messy bites.

Emma put her hand to her mouth like she was gonna throw up.

"You feeling all right?" I asked.

"You should've let me bury it."

"Why?"

"That bird just tore the other one apart!"

I shrugged. "She's gotta eat."

"Well, it's disgusting."

"Bet you don't look too pretty chewing your food up either."

Emma ignored me. "You shouldn't keep an eagle in a cage anyway. They're supposed to fly free. Poor bird."

"Poor bird?" I asked. "I just gave her a delicious supper."

"I wouldn't want a free supper if it meant I had to be locked up in a cage." She stroked the side of the cage with one finger, then gave me that look again.

I'd had just about enough. "Don't you look at me like I'm some old sow!"

Emma tipped her head like a confused dog. "An old what?"

"A pig! After I was nice enough to show you around."

"You weren't that nice," she snapped back. "You didn't warn me about the thorn bushes." She held up her scratched hands.

She had a point.

"Who's there?" a voice suddenly called out. We both took a step back. Big Foot came out onto his porch carrying a shotgun. Though it wasn't a Sunday, he wore a white shirt with a starched collar. Big Foot always had a clean shirt on, I'll give him that. Either Mrs. Pooley still did her son's laundry or she'd taught him to wash and iron them himself.

"It's me, Dit," I said. "I was just feeding your eagle."

Big Foot glanced at me, then looked Emma over. "You the new Negra girl?" he asked finally.

"Yes," said Emma.

"You say, 'Yes, sir,' to a white man around here."

Emma said nothing.

"Dit, I warned you about uppity Negras. That Elbert's bad enough. Don't you go being friends with this one too."

Elbert was a colored boy I went fishing with in the summer. Since Chip went to visit his grandma just about every year, I guess you could say Chip was my school friend and Elbert was my summer friend. But Elbert was fifteen, same age as my older brother Elman, who had recently started acting strange. Pa had taught him how to drive, and all at once, Elman was more interested in chores and crops and being responsible than in fooling around with the rest of us. I was worried the same thing was gonna happen to Elbert, which was why I'd been counting on the postmaster's son to be my backup.

"Aw, Big Foot," I said with a wave of my hand. "My mama's making me show her around. We ain't friends."

Big Foot nodded and went back inside. Me and Emma walked home. She was awful quiet. When we reached her house, she didn't even bother to say goodbye.

5

ELBERT AND DOC HALEY

IN MOUNDVILLE ALL THE LITTLE KIDS RAN together in the street playing kick the can, white and colored alike. The big kids played ball. Pa sometimes helped a colored neighbor with their fence and stayed for supper, and there was an old Negra woman Mama liked to quilt with now and then. There were no Negras at our church or school, but everybody sat in the rocking chairs on Mrs. Pooley's front porch. Only if all the chairs were taken and Big Foot or Mayor Davidson came by would one of the Negras jump up and lean against the railing instead.

My friend Elbert's pa was called Doc Haley, even though he was a barber, not a doctor. His shop was right on Main Street. All the men in town went to Doc Haley's shop, whites and Negras. There were two rooms—the front room where Doc cut hair and the back room where he and Elbert slept. The front room had a large barber chair, a shelf full of creams and tonics, a water basin and a small stove and table in the back corner where Doc and Elbert did their cooking. Elbert's mama had died when he was little, so Doc had gotten as good at frying fish as he was at giving haircuts.

About a week after Emma had arrived, I stopped by the shop to see Elbert. He was sitting in the barber chair while his father cut his hair. Elbert's hair was just as dark as Emma's, but his skin was a shade or two lighter.

"Sure," Elbert said when I asked if he wanted to go fishing. He moved to jump up from the chair, but Doc Haley put a hand on his shoulder.

"Just a minute, Elbert," Doc said. "You remember that talk we had about this summer?"

"Yes, Pa," said Elbert. He frowned. "Do we have to start right now?"

Doc Haley smiled. "No, I guess we don't. Go ahead. But tomorrow, we'll get to work."

When me and Elbert were settled on the bank of the Black Warrior with our fishing rods, I asked him what Doc had been talking about.

"Pa's gonna teach me how to give shaves and cut hair this summer," Elbert explained. "Says he ain't gonna live forever and the store'll be mine someday."

Back before I was born, Doc had been one of my pa's sharecroppers. We usually had four or five families working on our land. Instead of paying Pa money to use the land, they promised to give him part of their crops. Some people had a hard time getting sharecroppers because of the way they treated them, but Pa was honest and never had no trouble dividing up the profits at the end of each year.

Doc Haley had finally decided he was tired of sharecropping and he was gonna get himself some land of his own. Problem was, no one wanted to sell. He finally convinced my pa to give him a bit of land and some tools on credit. Pa always admired gumption. By the end of one year, Doc Haley had earned enough to pay Pa back every penny he owed him. "I ain't never seen a man work so hard," Pa said whenever he told the story. They became friends after that. Couple of years later, Doc Haley gave up farming and bought the barbershop.

"That's great," I said to Elbert, though I was a little jealous. My pa wasn't treating me like a man.

"Yeah." Elbert reeled in his line and threw it out again without looking at me. "'Cept it means I won't have as much time for fooling around. So I expect this'll be our last fishing trip for a while."

"Oh." I knew it. Just like Elman.

"Sorry, Dit."

I shrugged like I didn't mind. But I did. Elbert was patient and didn't talk much either. These two things together made him just about the perfect fishing partner. Inside, I cursed Emma again for being a girl. It was gonna be one lonely summer.

That afternoon I caught me four large catfish, and Elbert got only one. I was teasing him something awful as we walked back to his pa's shop. I usually traded fish for a trim, and it was about time for a haircut. Doc Haley had just invited me to stay for dinner when the bells on the front door jingled. We all looked up and saw Big Foot standing in the doorway.

"Afternoon, Mr. Big Foot, sir," said Doc Haley. "Would you like a haircut?"

"Nope." Big Foot looked around the room. Drinking had turned his nose permanently red, but his hair was still a nice shade of brown, even if it was a little uneven. I wondered if he cut it himself.

"How about a shave and a shoe shine?" Doc Haley was a

tall man, with short gray hair and a clean-shaven face. But today, he looked shorter than usual.

"No." Big Foot casually let his hand rest on the pistol on his belt.

"Then what can I do for you?" Doc's low voice cracked a little.

Big Foot picked up a bottle of hair tonic from the shelf.

"That's twenty-five cents, sir," said Doc brightly. "Right good tonic. Want me to ring it up for you?"

Big Foot just put that bottle of tonic in his pocket and walked right out of the store. I probably seen the same thing happen ten times before, but for some reason, I questioned it that day.

"Why you let Big Foot steal from you?" I asked.

Doc Haley ignored me till Big Foot turned the corner out of sight.

"Well, Dit, there is some things in life that are worth making a stink over," said Doc as he put the fish in a pan on the stove. "But a bottle of hair tonic ain't one of them."

6

THE BUZZARD

EMMA MADE GOOD ON HER PROMISE NOT to leave her front porch. She was just about always sitting in an old rocking chair, swaying back and forth and reading a book. The only book we owned was the family Bible, but every few days Emma had a new book that was a different color or thickness. Left one on her front step once. I crept over and snuck a peek. *Treasure Island,* by someone called Robert Louis Stevenson. Sounded kind of promising, but when I opened it up, there were no pictures, just words, words, words. I left it on the stoop.

When Emma wasn't reading, she was watching me. Which was awful annoying. She never said nothing, though, so I had almost gotten used to it till one day she called out, "Why are you carrying that gun?"

I turned around. I had my shotgun slung over my shoulder and was heading for the path into the woods. "Going hunting," I said. "I've gotta practice for the Fourth hunt."

"The Fourth of July was last week."

"I know that." I kept walking. That girl must have thought I was as stupid as a pumpkin. She'd seen me at the town celebration. I knew 'cause I caught her watching me give baby Robert and Lois a ride in my wagon, and I'd seen her watching the fireworks from the post office stoop. She'd looked kind of lonely.

Emma put her book aside and scrambled down her steps. "So what's the Fourth hunt?" She fell in step beside me, following me down the shaded path. I didn't have no choice but to answer.

"Every year on the Fourth of July, all the best hunters meet in front of Mrs. Pooley's store. They each pay two dollars to enter the contest. Then everyone has eight hours to go out and shoot all the squirrels, rabbits and birds they can. The person who brings back the most game wins all the money. I'm gonna win next year."

"Why do you want to win a stupid contest like that?" asked Emma.

"It's not stupid. My pa won the hunt twice when I was little, and Ulman once came in third."

"Who won this year?"

"Mr. Fulton, the town carpenter. Big Foot came in second and he was real mad."

Pa always talked about how winning the hunt had really been something. I was sure I was gonna win next year. Everyone said I had the best aim of anyone this side of the Mississippi. Give me a baseball, a stone or a shotgun—I could hit anything. If I could only find enough money to enter, my pa wouldn't call me "Della, Ollie, Ulman, Elman, Raymond, uh, I mean Dit" ever again.

"So why are you practicing now if the contest is already over?"

"I'm gonna enter next year. Gotta be at least thirteen."

"And where are you going to get two whole dollars?" asked Emma.

I hadn't quite figured that out myself. We went over a small bridge and walked along the river for a while. The woods were thick here, shading us from the hot July sun.

"You haven't shot anything yet," Emma broke the silence.

"That's 'cause I ain't seen no rabbits. I can kill any bird with my flip-it." At that moment, a huge low-flying buzzard appeared downriver.

"Couldn't kill that buzzard," said Emma.

The buzzard flew in lazy circles, eyeing a dead squirrel on the path about twenty feet in front of us. It came closer and closer till the bird hovered right above the squirrel.

I rolled my eyes. "Don't you know nothing? There's a big fine if you kill a buzzard. You could even go to jail." Wasn't quite sure if this was true. But Raymond said Elman knew someone whose brother's cousin had gone to jail for shooting a buzzard. So I wasn't taking no chances.

"I knew you couldn't do it," said Emma.

I raised the gun to my shoulder, and before I could think about that fine, I'd fired. The kickback of the weapon knocked me to the ground.

"Why'd you do that!" Emma yelled.

"You dared me."

The buzzard started flapping its wings wildly. I'd hit its right wing and it sank to the ground.

Emma pulled me up. The buzzard was blocking our path forward, so we turned and started to hurry back the way we had come. But an ugly switching noise seemed to follow us. I looked back.

With a last burst of strength, the buzzard had forced itself back into the air. It flew right over our heads, so low I could feel its dirty feathers brush my forehead. Emma shrieked and the buzzard fell to the ground, not five feet from where we were standing.

The bird lay still, a pile of wrinkled feathers and skin.

"Is it dead?" Emma whispered.

I didn't know, but now it was blocking our path home. I took a step toward it. The bird jumped up and let out a terrible scream.

Now, I'm no coward, but you got to understand, a buzzard's got a beak on him like the jaws of a bear. So I did what any sensible person would do—ran as fast as I could in the opposite direction. Emma was right behind me. The gun slapped at my leg, but I didn't stop. Took us a quite a while to get home 'cause we had to circle the long way round through the broom sage patch where the rabbits like to run. Saw a ton of rabbits too, but I didn't feel like hunting anymore. Emma glanced at the shotgun once but didn't say a word.

When we finally made it back, Mama and Mrs. Walker were sewing in the lot between our houses. "Where have you two been?" Mama asked.

Before I could think up a good lie, something started roaring, like a lion way off in the distance.

Mama looked up. "What's that?"

The sound came from the sky. Far off, we could see a black dot coming toward us.

I whispered to Emma, "Think it's the buzzard?"

But it wasn't. The noise got louder and louder. Finally, Mrs. Walker put down her sewing and said, "It's an airplane."

A moment later, a small single-engine plane flew directly over us. I knew what a plane was, of course. We had all read about it in the paper. But as far as I knew, no one in Mound-ville had ever seen one. Till now. It was like magic—a metal box, soaring overhead like an eagle. The plane was flying so low, we could see the pilot lean over and wave at us.

Emma laughed and waved back. I was just relieved it wasn't the buzzard.

7

THE FISHING TRIP

EVERY SUMMER, PA TAKES ME FISHING. I look forward to this trip all year since it's just about the only time I get to talk to Pa all by myself. I was so excited I could barely concentrate as I packed all the supplies. Ulman and Raymond said thirteen was the year Pa gave you the man-to-man talk. My birthday wasn't until February, but I figured Pa might forget and give me the talk a little early.

The morning of our trip dawned crisp and clear—the perfect day for a fishing trip. We didn't get a real early start 'cause Pa had been up half the night nursing a sick cow, but we set off right after breakfast. We were going to my favorite fishing hole, a short drive from town.

Pa had a Model T Ford, with a cloth top to put up when it rained. There were only three cars in town: my pa had one, Dr. Griffith had one to help him make his rounds and Mayor Davidson bought a car 'cause he couldn't stand to be outdone by anyone. Pa kept promising to teach me to drive just as soon as he got a chance.

We had to follow a dirt track off the main road to get to the fishing hole. You had to know where it was or you'd never find it. So my jaw just about fell off its hinges when we drove up to the riverbank and found Emma and her daddy sitting on a log.

"What are you doing here?" I yelled as I scrambled out of the car.

"Dit," Pa said sharply.

"We're fishing," said Emma. She clutched the fishing rod with both hands.

"How'd you ever find this place?" asked Pa.

Mr. Walker cast out his line. I could tell he knew how to fish, even if his daughter didn't. "I asked Dr. Griffith to recommend a good fishing hole, and he brought us here."

"Oh," Pa replied.

"He drove into Selma for the day and dropped us off," Mr. Walker explained.

"I see," said Pa.

"As a boy, I did a lot of fishing. I wanted to show Emma what it was like. Seems like you had the same idea with your son."

Me and Pa stood there for a long moment. I waited for Pa to tell them to leave. "Well," Pa said slowly, "there's plenty of fish here for all of us."

So much for my man-to-man talk.

We sat down on the old log that stretched across the creek. Pa and Mr. Walker each sat on one end of the log. Me and Emma were in the middle, far enough apart so we wouldn't accidentally bump into each other.

No one moved for a long time.

"Well," Pa said finally. "How's it working out at the post office?"

"Just fine, sir," said Mr. Walker.

Pa chuckled. "No need to call me sir. Though there is some men in town who stand on ceremony."

Mr. Walker nodded. "Dr. Griffith told me."

"I'm not sure why we need a lawman myself," said Pa. "In a town this small seems we should be able to manage things ourselves. But others felt differently, and, well, there we are."

Mr. Walker nodded again.

"I just don't want you to have any trouble," Pa said. "I like getting my mail on time."

Mr. Walker finally smiled then. "I heard the last postman had a few shortcomings."

"A few shortcomings? Shoot, the only thing that was short about him was the time he worked each day."

Mr. Walker grinned again. "Glad to hear I'm doing better."

Maybe it wouldn't be such a bad day after all, even if I didn't get my talk. A moment later Emma's pole began to jerk and wiggle.

"I caught a fish!" squealed Emma.

She tried to reel in the line but didn't know how. I grabbed the pole to help.

"Let me do it!" she protested.

But I already had the fish out of the water. It was a large perch. "Where's the net?" I asked as the fish squirmed wildly in the air.

"I thought you brought it," Pa said.

I guess I should've done a better job packing.

"I always just use some extra line to string up the fish," said Mr. Walker.

I looked around. "Don't need it," I said. "There's a rocky pool under that bridge. Fish can't get out of that." I picked up the squirming fish and dropped it into the pool.

Problem solved. For a while, the fish were coming as fast as we could pull them in. Pa got a big perch, and then Mr. Walker caught a huge catfish. I caught one of each and Emma reeled in a small carp all by herself.

She proudly slid off the log and walked under the small footbridge. She dumped the fish into the pool and then leaned over to look in the water.

But there weren't no other fish in the pool. Her fish swam around a bit dazed. "The other fish got away," she said.

"Couldn't have," said Mr. Walker. "Take another look."

Emma leaned over again. Now her fish was gone too 'cept for its tail sticking out of the end of a large water moccasin.

The water moccasin is a dark snake with a yellow stomach, a triangular head and slitty eyes like a cat. It's poisonous, and once its jaws snap shut, it don't let go. It's sometimes called a cottonmouth 'cause when its mouth is open, the flesh inside its throat is as white as cotton. The water moccasin is more aggressive than most snakes and territorial too. And we had invaded its home.

Emma didn't know all this. But she did know enough to scream, "Snakes!"

I ain't never seen a man move so fast. Mr. Walker jumped up and stomped to the edge of the pool. Sure enough, there were no fish, but five large water moccasins were slithering out of the water.

Before me or Pa could move, Mr. Walker pulled out a pistol and fired. Emma put her hands over her ears and ran back toward the log.

Guess Mr. Walker didn't fire a pistol too often back in Boston 'cause even though he was only a foot away, he didn't hit none of the snakes. Course it is awful hard to kill a snake by shooting—the best way is to just take an ax and chop off its head. I would have told him this, but before I could, Mr. Walker fired again. The bullet bounced off a rock and the noise scared the snakes. They slunk back into the darkness of the pool.

Emma ran over and hugged her pa. Mr. Walker was breathing hard as he put down the gun.

"What you doing shooting off that pistol?" demanded Pa.

"Protecting my daughter," said Mr. Walker.

"You didn't even hit none of those old cottonmouths. Only a fool bring along a gun when he don't know how to use it."

"Don't you call me a fool!" Mr. Walker snapped.

"What you gonna do, wave your gun at me?" asked Pa.

"Don't be mean to my daddy!" said Emma.

"Shut up," I said. "If my pa calls him a fool, he's a fool."

We all began to yell at once till we sounded like a chicken house when a fox has broken in. A huge crack of thunder shut us up. Soon as I looked at the sky, it began to pour.

Pa gave a great sigh. "I think we'd all best go home."

By the time we had all the supplies back in the car, it was raining cats and dogs. If I didn't know better, I'd say there were a few mules and pigs in there too. Mr. Walker sat in the front with Pa, and me and Emma climbed in the back. We put up the top on Pa's Model T, but we all got soaked anyway. Every once in a while there'd be a flash of lightning and we'd be able to see clearly for a second or two. Then the thunder would come with a loud clap and everything would turn dark again.

Pa suddenly slammed on the brakes, causing me and Emma to fall hard against the front seat. When the lightning flashed again, we saw a huge tree blocking the road, only inches from the hood of our car. There was no way around it.

Pa banged hard on the steering wheel. Mr. Walker just shook his head.

"At least it missed the car," said Emma.

"What we gonna do now?" I asked.

Pa thought for a moment. "Jim Dang-It lives about half a mile from here. He'll put us up." So we climbed out of the car and started walking.

Jim Dang-It was an eccentric old man, half colored and half Indian. He lived in the woods all alone and wouldn't take no help from no one, not even if all his tobacco crop washed away. Said he'd rather eat acorns like the squirrels than be beholden to a white man. But even though he wouldn't take no help, he was more than happy to give it. He had saved many folks who had gotten lost in the woods. Even though I knew all about him, I'd never dared go to his place. He was the only Negra I knew who could bawl out a white man and not get hurt.

We were all feeling pretty low as we trudged down the muddy path. All except Emma. Despite the rain, she strolled along like it was a sunny spring day. Once or twice, I even caught her whistling. When I finally asked her why, for goodness' sake, wasn't she in a foul mood like the rest of us, she only asked, "Is fishing always this exciting?" I didn't answer.

We were wetter than a school of catfish by the time we reached Jim's cabin. Pa pounded on his door.

"What you folks doing out in this dang weather?" Jim Dang-It barked at us as he pulled open the door. He was a small man but covered in muscles. "Come on in."

The four of us crowded into his tiny cabin. Dr. Griffith was standing by the fire. He smiled broadly as Emma and Mr. Walker walked in. "Sure am glad to see you two. I was on my way to see if you needed a ride when my car got stuck in the mud."

Dr. Griffith was the only doctor in Moundville. He had a full gray beard and brown eyes that didn't scold you even if you did something stupid like jump off the roof of the barn. (Raymond dared me. It wasn't my fault.) Dr. Griffith just patched you up and sent you home, and for that, I liked him.

Jim Dang-It took Emma's wet jacket and draped it over a chair in front of the fire. "Dr. Griffith worried himself sick about you." He brought me and Emma a blanket. "What kind of dang fools go out when there's a storm coming?"

"I didn't see no signs of a storm," I said.

"No signs of a storm!" exclaimed Jim. "What do they teach you kids these days? Didn't you notice the squirrels hiding and hear the birds singing their storm song?"

"No," I said.

"Dang stupid," said Jim. But he smiled as he shook his head.

Jim's cabin was nothing like I had imagined. Sure, there was a dirt floor, but it was swept neat as Mama's. There was a bed built into one corner and covered with a bright-colored quilt. His tools were neatly hung on the walls. Every item had its place. A pot of coffee boiled over the open fireplace.

There wasn't no place for all of us to sleep, so Emma got the bed and I settled down with a blanket on the floor. Pa, Mr. Walker, Dr. Griffith and Jim Dang-It huddled around the fireplace, sipping coffee.

"All this rain," said Pa. "Ain't doing my corn no good."

"More rain coming," said Dr. Griffith.

34

Mr. Walker nodded. "Rain all over the state, from what I hear."

They were all silent for a moment. Jim Dang-It seemed to be studying Mr. Walker. "You the new postmaster, right?" Jim asked finally.

"Yes, I am," said Mr. Walker.

"Don't get too much mail myself," said Jim Dang-It. He blew on his coffee. "Anyone tell you 'bout that man in Selma?"

"I did," said Dr. Griffith.

"Good," said Jim. "'Cause it'd be a dang shame if . . ."

"Jim." Pa cut him off and gestured toward me and Emma.

"Sorry, kids," said Jim. "Know you're trying to sleep." He lowered his voice and continued talking. I listened real hard, but I couldn't quite make out what he was saying. I was just 'bout ready to roll over and go to sleep, when I felt a hand on my shoulder.

"Dit?"

I looked up. Emma had the quilt pulled up over her head and was peering out at me like a squirrel in its den.

"What?" I asked.

"This was the best fishing trip I've ever been on," said Emma.

"Ain't it the only fishing trip you've ever been on?"

"Well, yes," Emma admitted.

"And we lost all the fish," I grumbled.

"But didn't we have fun catching them?"

"No," I lied.

"Oh, come on, Dit." Emma laughed. "You were having a nice time before those snakes showed up."

"I was not!"

"You two still awake?" Mr. Walker interrupted. "Go to sleep."

I finally closed my eyes and the next thing I knew, the sun was up and Pa was pouring me a cup of coffee.

We had to drag the tree out of the road and dig out Dr. Griffith's car before we could go home. I was covered in mud by the time we were all done. As I handed my shovel back to Jim Dang-It, he turned to my pa and said, "Strong boy you got there."

Pa nodded. "Yup."

Guess it wasn't such a bad trip after all.

8

MAMA'S RULE

DIDN'T SEE MUCH OF EMMA FOR A WHILE
after that. She'd been okay on the fishing trip, and maybe we'd
even had a little fun, but I still didn't want to be her friend.
What'd we have in common? I loved the outdoors; she liked
to sit on the porch all day. But my mama had a rule—we didn't
have to like anyone, but we had to be nice to everyone. That's
exactly the kind of rule grown-ups make up, ain't it?

There was one place in town where everyone followed
Mama's rule—on the baseball field. Course it wasn't a real
field, just a vacant lot, but we used old rags to mark the bases
and even piled up some dirt to make a pitcher's mound. Everyone played, and I mean everyone: boys, girls, black, white,
green or orange, we all took our turn at bat.

One day in the beginning of August, it was so hot the sweat
dripped into my ears. We were picking teams when I noticed
Emma lurking on the edge of the field. She had a book in one
hand but wasn't reading. I was captain that day and was in a
good mood, having already gotten Raymond, Ulman and Pearl
for my side. There weren't too many people left, but that still

don't explain why I suddenly heard myself call out, "I pick Emma."

"Who?" asked Elbert. He had a rare afternoon off from working with his pa at the barbershop.

"Emma," I repeated. "Emma Walker. She's right over there." I pointed. Everyone turned to look.

Emma stood perfectly still, her eyes wide. "No thank you," she said finally, "I don't want to play."

Now this irritated me to no end. She'd been looking at us like we were enjoying a royal banquet and she ain't ate in a week. I knew she was lying. "Come on, Emma," I coaxed.

Emma glared at me, but she came over and joined our team.

Soon as I started pitching, I forgot all about her. I'm always the pitcher. No one can throw like me. I'm a fair hitter too, but pitching is what I do best. I think it comes from killing all those birds with my flip-it. Or maybe from the fact that I'm left-handed. Or maybe it was just 'cause I was the only one in town with a real glove.

Anyway, an hour later, Pearl was playing second base and Ulman was on first. Raymond was catching and taking his turn as umpire. Emma was somewhere way out in right field. I threw a fastball. Elbert swung and missed.

"Strike one," said Raymond.

I threw a curveball. Elbert swung and missed.

"Strike two," cried Raymond.

I threw another fastball, but Elbert hit it this time. He ran easily past first, but Pearl had her eye on the ball. She had to dive for it, but she caught it. I was pretty darn proud of my little sister. That made two outs.

Elman was up to bat next. I grinned at my older brother

in friendly competition. He hit my second pitch way out to right field and started running. The ball was falling directly toward Emma. All she had to do was reach out her hands and the ball would fall right into them. But Emma was staring at her fingernails.

The ball thumped into the dirt six inches from where Emma stood. She jumped.

"Pick it up!" I yelled. "Throw it to third!"

Elman was running slowly around the bases, laughing.

Emma picked up the ball like it was a wild rat about to bite her. She threw it with all her might. The ball went about ten feet. Toward Ulman on first. Elman slid into home.

I threw my glove to the ground and marched over to Emma. "What were you doing?" I snapped. "That should have been an easy out!"

"Sorry," she mumbled.

"Don't you know how to throw a ball?"

Emma shook her head. Her eyes welled up, but she didn't make a sound.

I felt a little bad then. "I gotta go back and pitch."

It started raining as I walked back to the mound. Mitch was up to bat next. He was the largest boy in the game, seventeen years old and at least 160 pounds. His face was slightly flat and he always wore a wide, lopsided grin. Dr. Griffith had some fancy name for his condition, but we just called him slow.

I threw a wicked curveball. Mitch hit it through the drizzle all the way to Main Street.

"Way to go!" Pearl called out. Raymond gave Mitch a push to start him running. Pretty soon everyone was chanting, "Mitch! Mitch!" as he took his victory lap around the bases.

Mitch's grin was wider than ever. He shook his head back

and forth as the rain came down and he joined in the chant. "Mitch! Mitch!" he yelled. "Way to go!"

Finally Mitch slid into home plate, splattering Raymond with mud. Everyone laughed.

"Watch where you're going!" Raymond grumbled.

This only made Mitch grin harder.

I glanced over at Emma. Even she was smiling a little. And suddenly I was glad I had asked her to play, even if it meant we lost the game.

Maybe there was something to Mama's rule.

9

THROWING STONES

IT FINALLY STOPPED RAINING THAT EVE-
ning after supper, and I went to hang out on Mrs. Pooley's
front porch. Doc Haley sat in one of the rockers, while me and
Elbert played marbles in the mud. It was a nice, quiet evening,
with no one saying much. After a game and a half, Big Foot
wandered out of the store onto his mama's front porch. Soon
as Doc saw him, he jumped up.

"Come on, Elbert," Doc said.

"I'm right in the middle of a game," Elbert protested.

"Sorry, son. It's time to go."

Me and Elbert divvied up our marbles, and he and Doc
went on home.

Big Foot sat down in the empty chair without saying a
word.

I headed home soon after that. It was already dark. The
moon was out, so I could see just fine to practice my pitching,
which I did by throwing rocks at each of the houses I passed.
I'd pick a spot, maybe ten inches square, above a door or between two windows and throw the rock at it. I'd heard once

that was how the great pitcher Walter Johnson had perfected his aim, and ever since, I'd practiced that way myself.

I hit Dr. Griffith's place first. He'd moved to town five or six years ago and his wife died two years after that, so now he lived alone in their large wooden house. The oak front door made a nice *thwunk* when my rock hit it.

Next to Dr. Griffith's house was a smaller house that he rented out to the schoolteacher. We had only one teacher in our primary school, which went from first to eighth grade. As far back as anyone could remember, the teacher had been Mr. Summons. But the old man had finally died—choked on a fish bone while he was eating his supper. His housekeeper found him, a pile of ungraded papers under his head.

So Mrs. Seay had recently moved into the house. She was a young widow from a rich family who had been educated at the University of Alabama. Most people said she wouldn't be a schoolteacher for long; she was too pretty not to get married again. I hadn't met her yet but had heard Mama gossiping about her. So I crept up to the window to see what she was like.

I guess she hadn't had time to hang her curtains 'cause I could see her clearly, reading by the fireside. She sure was pretty. Her long blond hair was braided and pinned high up on her head. Her dress had lace all over it and looked more suited to a fancy party than sitting at home reading a book. Round her neck she wore a string of pearls.

I could even see the book she was reading: *Democracy and Education,* by one John Dewey. What kind of foolishness was that? Ain't no democracy in school. Everyone knows that. The teacher is boss and if you forget that, you're gonna end up with one sore bottom.

I'd seen enough, so I moved a couple of steps back and took

aim at a little dark patch on the wood above her window. I pulled my arm back. Then right before I let the stone fly, Emma stepped out of the darkness.

It was exactly the wrong moment to surprise me: too late for me to stop my throw, but early enough to distract me. Instead of bouncing harmlessly off the wood, the rock sailed through the closed window, shattering the glass.

We both winced and ran for the bushes. Peeking through the leaves, we could see Mrs. Seay pick up a kerosene lamp and walk toward the front door. The door opened and she stepped outside. "Who's there?" she called sharply. Her long dress billowed in the night breeze.

Emma took a deep breath, like she was gonna say something, but I grabbed her shoulder. She shut up. Mrs. Seay walked right by the bush where we were hiding, scanned the yard twice, then went back inside.

I let out a sigh of relief and let my grip on Emma relax. She squirmed away. "You shouldn't be throwing rocks at people's houses."

"It's your fault," I spit back at her. "If you hadn't startled me, I wouldn't have broke her window."

"You have to go tell her what you did."

"No!" I whispered through clenched teeth. "Are you crazy?"

"Then I will." She brushed a clump of wet dirt off her dress.

"Emma, you can't tell," I pleaded.

"Why not?"

"I'm saving money for the Fourth hunt. I can't afford to pay for a broken window."

"Should have thought of that before you broke it." Emma stood up and looked over toward the front door.

"I'll tell everyone you're a snitch."

"So?" Emma replied.

"None of the kids will want to play with you."

"None of the kids play with me anyway."

"I do."

"Only 'cause your mama makes you."

I wanted to say that wasn't true, but it was. So I finally just said, "Please don't tell."

Emma pretended to mull it over, but I think she already had the whole thing worked out in her head. "Teach me to throw a ball and I won't tell."

"Emma," I sighed. "You ain't no good at baseball."

"I want to learn."

I shook my head.

"Fine." She started toward Mrs. Seay's front door.

"Wait," I said.

Emma paused. "Teach me to throw a ball," she repeated, "and I'll keep your secret."

I looked up at the broken window. Mrs. Seay was inside, sweeping up the glass shards. I looked back at Emma and nodded.

The next day, me and Emma spent hours on the banks of the Black Warrior River, throwing small smooth stones. "I don't want to learn to throw stones," Emma protested. "I want to throw a baseball."

"You gotta learn how to keep your eye on the ball," I explained. "And how to throw and how to aim. And the best way to learn all that is by skipping stones."

She didn't complain no more after that.

My stones would skip across the water like they was flying. Hers would fall in the water with a loud *ker-plunk*.

But I gotta give her one thing. That girl was stubborn. I tried for three hours to show her how it was done, and she never got more than one skip. I thought that was the end of it. If my friend Chip didn't catch on to something right away, he called it stupid and gave up.

So I was surprised when Emma came over the next day. She watched us weed the vegetable garden till Mama stopped and asked her what she wanted. "Dit was teaching me to skip stones yesterday, Mrs. Sims."

"Did you get the hang of it?" Mama asked, wiping her hands on her apron.

"No, Mrs. Sims. It was my first time, since I wasn't allowed to go down to the river by myself in Boston."

"Well, then," said Mama, "sounds like you need yourself another lesson."

Three more hours on the riverbank and Emma's stones still fell flat into the water. The whole thing seemed pointless to me. I knew there was no way Emma was ever gonna learn how to skip stones. But I didn't want her to tell on me, so I guess I had to keep trying to teach her. Sooner or later, she'd decide to give up on her own.

"You're getting it," I lied.

"No, I'm not," said Emma.

"You're not holding the stones right," I said for the fifth time.

"Show me again," said Emma.

So I took her hand in mine and wrapped it around a smooth flat stone. Her fingers were cool and stiff, but her skin was beautiful, kind of like the mud in a creek after a hard rain. I rubbed her hands between mine, trying to get the blood running. She watched me. Then I said, "Try it again."

She took that stone and threw it so hard, it skipped seven or eight times across the water. We both stood there with our mouths open. I'm not sure who was more surprised.

"Oh, Dit, you did it!" she exclaimed. "You taught me to throw stones."

"I didn't do nothing," I said. "You figured it out yourself."

But it sure made me feel good that she'd said it. And I started to do some thinking. Taking Emma to the top of my mound hadn't gotten rid of her. She hadn't cried on the fishing trip, not even when we had to walk through the rain and the mud to Jim Dang-It's. Now Emma had gone and learned how to skip stones when I had thought she couldn't. Maybe there was other stuff I was wrong about too. Maybe Emma was someone who'd make a good friend.

While I was thinking and wondering, Emma picked up another stone and threw it as hard as she could. It fell into the water with a loud *ker-plunk*. She just laughed and picked up another stone. This one skipped four or five times. Emma let out a delighted scream.

We stood there till the sun went down, skipping stones.

10

THE CAVE

EMMA SURE WASN'T LIKE NO OTHER GIRL I'd ever met. She told me about museums she had visited in Boston and had a set of paints like a real artist. Emma didn't approve of sneaking into places, unless it was the Negra church so she could play the organ. She used to have piano lessons at her school in Boston and had a book of songs by people like Bach and Mozart. She said they were from faraway places like Germany and Austria. I pointed out that we were at war with Germany and she shouldn't aid the enemy by playing their music. "How is playing their music going to aid them?" Emma asked. I didn't have no answer, and the music was kind of pretty, so I just sat back and listened.

It's not like Emma knew everything. In some ways, she was plumb stupid. She had never built a fort or played hide-and-seek in the woods. When we decided to dig a secret hideout in one of the mounds, I had to show her everything.

We weren't working two minutes till Emma started complaining. "I'm getting blisters," she said, staring at her hand.

"You're holding the shovel wrong." I came over and showed

her where to place her hands. She tried scooping up some more dirt with the shovel.

"Better?" I asked.

"I think so."

"Good. But you're still gonna get blisters."

I showed Emma how to spread out the dirt on the side of the mound so it didn't make a huge bulge or fall down in big clumps. If we were gonna have a secret hideout, we couldn't have everyone knowing where it was.

After an hour of work, I was covered with dirt and had to lie down in the tall grass to rest. But Emma was working at the same slow pace, looking like she had just bathed for church. "Did you ever build a cave back in Boston?" I asked.

"No," said Emma. "There wasn't anywhere like this. We lived in a row house."

"What's that?" I asked.

"A bunch of houses built next to each other so that they share walls. You can get a whole bunch of row houses on one city block. Maybe nine or ten."

"Nine or ten houses on one block?" I asked.

Emma shrugged. "Maybe more. There were always people around, sitting outside on their front porches, visiting. Kind of like people do at Mrs. Pooley's store."

I thought for a moment. "Guess there'd be a lot of people to play with."

"Yeah," said Emma quietly. "And a lot of noise too."

"What if you need a little peace and quiet?"

"I'd go to my room and read a book."

"Didn't you have a tree to sit in? Or a field to run around in?"

"There was a park across town. But we had to take the

streetcar there. And Mama didn't like me to go alone. And it cost a dime."

I imagined having to pay a dime every time I wanted to see a tree or look at the sky or just be still and listen to my thoughts. If I had to live in one of those row houses, maybe I'd take up reading too.

11

ROOT BEER AND HARDTACK

IT TOOK ME AND EMMA ABOUT A WEEK, but we finally had the cave big enough so that we could both crawl inside. We went to the riverbank and picked up two large stones and used them to pack the walls hard and smooth. Sunlight trickled in through the vines we had woven together for the door, making shapes of light on the dirt floor.

"Know what would make this absolutely perfect?" I asked.

"What?"

"A bottle of soda," I said.

"How about a whole case of soda?" Emma suggested. "It'd stay cold in the cave."

I thought this over. I had a couple of dimes at home and almost a whole year to save for the Fourth hunt.

"We can split the cost," Emma continued. "Mama gave me some money when we took that train down from Boston."

I nodded. "Sounds good to me."

Me and Emma ran home to get our money. I picked up my wagon to pull the soda in and we headed on over to Mrs. Pooley's store. When we got there, Big Foot was sitting in one of the rocking chairs, his feet propped up on an empty box.

"Well, if it ain't Dit and his nigger girl." He took another sip of his beer.

I didn't know what to do. I'd heard Big Foot call colored folks in our town names before, but not right to their face. "Hello, Big Foot," I said.

Emma didn't say anything.

"Ain't your mama trained you right," Big Foot said to Emma. "A white man speak to you, you say hello."

"Hello," mumbled Emma, then turned to me. "I'm going inside."

I waved bye to Big Foot and followed Emma inside. Found her standing in the back of the store, staring at her shoes. "You all right?" I asked.

"I don't like that man," Emma said.

"Nobody likes him much."

Emma said nothing.

"Cream or root beer?" I asked.

"What?"

"What kind of soda you like?"

"Root beer," Emma said.

"Me too," I said, and handed her my dime.

Emma paid Mrs. Pooley for the soda while I loaded the case into my wagon. We went out the back door, just in case Big Foot was still there. On the way back to the mound, Emma suggested we stop at the post office and say hi to her daddy.

That was fine with me. Mr. Walker sometimes asked me and Emma to help him sort the mail. Emma thought this was

51

boring, but I kind of liked it. Besides, the post office was right next to the train depot, and I was always up for a little train watching.

Soon as we entered, Mr. Walker looked up from his record book and grinned. "Boy, I sure am glad to see you two. My leg is hurting something awful today. Think you could stay a while and help me sort the mail?"

"Sure," I said. Mr. Walker found Emma a sharp knife while I dragged the mailbag over to the corner with the mailboxes. Emma slit open the bag and we started pulling out piles of letters, bills and catalogs. We had to put everything into the right mailbox. My family's was number 14. I got into a rhythm while I worked—glance at the letter, see the number, stick it in the box. Found it kind of relaxing.

But Emma was awful quiet. "You okay?" I asked.

"Of course." Emma kept sorting the letters into piles.

Was she still upset about Big Foot? Should I have said something to him when he was nasty to her back at the store? I wanted to ask her what she thought, but I wasn't sure if that'd make things worse. Mr. Walker was still standing across the room by the front counter, so finally I just lowered my voice and asked, "What happened to your daddy's leg?"

"I don't want to talk about it."

Before I could press her about it, my pa came into the post office. He and Mr. Walker had been friendly since the fishing trip, and I thought maybe he was stopping by just to say hello.

"Hi, Pa!" I cried out.

Pa hardly looked at me as he rushed over to the counter where Mr. Walker was working.

"Do you have the new Sears and Roebuck catalog?" Pa didn't say hello to Mr. Walker either, but that only made me feel a little better.

"Yes," Mr. Walker said, reaching into his desk and pulling it out. "Is something wrong?"

"Thank goodness," said Pa, wiping his forehead with his sleeve. "Can you place an order by telegraph? There's been so much rain, half my corn is rotting in the field. I thought if I got some more seed by next week, I might be able to—"

"The corn is rotting?" I asked.

Pa glanced over at me. "Uh, hello, Ulman."

"Dit," I corrected.

"Yes, Dit, of course." He flipped through the catalog Mr. Walker handed him until he found the right page. "This is what I need."

"Let me get the form," said Mr. Walker.

"Are we gonna starve, Pa?" I asked as Mr. Walker was searching for the correct form.

"What?" Pa kept his eyes on the catalog.

"If you don't get that seed, are we gonna starve?"

"No, course not," said Pa. "Might not be able to send Ollie to that teaching college she's got her eye on, but we won't starve."

"Found it," said Mr. Walker, picking a pen up off the counter. "Now just tell me what you want it to say."

"But if we don't have no corn," I continued, "how we gonna feed the cows, pigs and chickens?"

"Dit, I don't have time to answer all your little questions." He turned to Mr. Walker. "How many words do I get for fifty cents?"

"I'm working," I muttered under my breath, but Pa didn't hear me. Emma did and opened her mouth to say something, but just then a train whistle blew.

Trains passed through Moundville six times a day: 7 a.m., 9 a.m., 12 noon, 4 p.m., 7 p.m. and 9 p.m. The post office clock said it was almost four thirty now, so it couldn't be one of the trains on the daily schedule. I glanced out the window. The train wasn't stopping, just chugging slowly through the station. A man stuck his head out of a train car window and hollered, "We're off to get Kaiser Bill!"

"It's packed with soldiers," I cried as I put down the mail I was sorting. "Come on!"

Me and Emma ran out of the post office and over to the train depot. The United States had just entered the Great War, and I guess the soldiers were getting ready to ship out. The soldiers waved like crazy when they saw me and Emma on the platform.

"Good luck!" Emma yelled, and waved.

"Show those Germans what's what!" I added.

A young man with a shaved head poked his head out the window and cried, "We'll be home by Christmas!" Then he threw something out the window.

It was a thick, round cracker. Pretty soon the others were throwing them too, and by the time the train had made it through the station, the platform was covered with crackers.

Emma ran back to get an old mailbag and Mr. Walker came back with her to help us gather them up. My father wasn't with him. I put a cracker in my mouth and bit down. "Ow!" I said. "It's as hard as a piece of wood."

Mr. Walker laughed. "It's hardtack, Dit. Never goes bad, so the soldiers carry it with them in their packs. Can't even break it with a hammer, but if you soak it in your mouth or in a pot of water, it'll slowly dissolve."

"Why'd they throw it to us?" asked Emma.

Mr. Walker shrugged. "It's good luck."

So me and Emma added that bag of hardtack to my wagon. Planned to store it in our cave along with the soda. Figured if Pa didn't get his seed in time and we got real hungry, I could take some home and gnaw at it, like a dog on a bone.

12

THE BOWL

THE SUN WAS STARTING TO GO DOWN BY the time we finally got the wagon full of root beer and hardtack back to our cave. Walking up and down the mound so many times had carved a little path into the side, but it was still hard hauling the wagon up between all the prickly bushes.

When we finally reached the entrance to our cave and shoved all the soda and crackers inside, we realized it wasn't quite as large as we'd thought 'cause there was now barely enough room for the two of us. So the next day we returned with our shovels and picks and set about making the cave bigger. We hadn't been digging long when Emma gasped.

"What's wrong?" I asked. "You pop a blister again?" This had caused quite a bit of upset the week before.

"No," Emma scoffed. "I found something. A bowl."

We both crawled out of the cave to look at the bowl in the sunlight. It was shaped like a pumpkin with a wide stem 'cept it was covered with a shiny black glaze. There was a picture on one side. I brushed away some of the dirt.

A drawing of a hand with an eye in the middle of the palm was scratched into the pottery.

"What does it mean?" asked Emma, pressing her palm up against the one on the bowl.

I shrugged. Her hand was exactly the same size as the drawing.

"Let's go ask Jim Dang-It," said Emma. "He's half Indian, isn't he?"

So off we went.

"What you dang kids up to?" Jim asked when we arrived at his cabin. He was outside cutting branches from a low-hanging tree.

"We found this," said Emma, holding up the bowl. "Can you tell us what it is?"

Jim Dang-It dropped his handsaw and took the bowl from Emma. He cradled it in his arms like a baby. He traced his fingertips over the drawing, then turned the bowl slowly in his hands. He held the bowl up to his eyes and peeked inside. He blew a short breath into the bowl, then put it to his ear to listen. Finally, he put the bowl down on his front stoop and took a step back. "This dang thing," he said slowly, "is a sign."

"A sign of what?" asked Emma.

"This bowl was used by the Indians. When someone died, they filled it with water and placed it in the fire so that their loved one would not go thirsty on their journey to the underworld. The hand and the eye stand for the God who made everything and the God who sees everything."

Emma listened wide-eyed. I was more interested in the fact that this was the first time I'd ever heard Jim say more than a word or two without saying *dang*.

"You found this dang bowl on the very anniversary of my wife's death." He shook his head. "It's a sign."

"A sign of what?" I repeated Emma's question.

Jim Dang-It ignored me. He had Emma hold the bowl as he carefully filled it with water. Then he ordered me to pick up the green branches he had been cutting and told us both to follow him.

Jim led us to the top of one of the mounds. There was a pile of wood already gathered there and a small, folded blanket. He knelt down and began to build a fire.

"What are you doing?" asked Emma politely, still clutching the bowl.

"My wife died fifteen years ago today. This is how I show her that I love and miss her." Jim closed his eyes, and his lips moved briefly in a silent prayer.

When the fire was burning well, Jim Dang-It had me throw the green branches on top of it. Soon the fire began giving off a thick stream of smoke. Jim unfolded the blanket and held it over the fire. Every so often, he'd snap it quickly away, sending a clear smoke signal up to the heavens.

This went on for a long time. Finally, Jim Dang-It put down the blanket and nodded at Emma. She stepped forward and gave him the bowl. He carefully placed it into the center of the small fire. The flames hissed as a bit of water sloshed over the side.

"We leave the bowl there until all the water is gone." Jim smiled. "My wife will be so pleased you gave her this gift."

I hadn't meant to give that bowl to Jim Dang-It and his dead wife. I'd wanted to keep it. Or at least sell it to someone and make a little money for the Fourth hunt. It wasn't fair. Emma found the bowl; if I didn't get it, then she should. Seemed like a waste just to burn it up.

No one said much as we walked home. I was too busy thinking. Pottery was made under great heat. Putting it in a little fire like that probably wouldn't harm it at all. I decided when the fire had burned out and the bowl had cooled, I'd sneak back and take it.

But the next day when I returned to the top of the mound, the bowl was gone. Jim must have gone back to get it. He was half Indian. Maybe one of his relatives had made that bowl, a long, long time ago. Maybe it was right for his dead wife to have it after all.

13

SHOES, SWIMMING AND WORMS

EVERY EVENING BEFORE BED, MAMA MADE us wash our feet in a bucket of cold water. Della and Ollie were practically grown-up girls now, so they usually wore shoes and helped Ma in the house, but the rest of us just about always went around barefoot. Who wanted to bother with shoes, especially in summer? They just got dirty when you were swimming in the river or playing ball.

Emma, of course, always wore shoes and kept her dress neat and tidy too. Mama liked her. I would have been glad they got along if Mama hadn't kept asking why she couldn't have had one child, "just one child!" more like Emma.

One hot August afternoon, me and Pearl decided to teach Emma to swim, so the three of us started walking down to the swimming hole. Emma had put on her oldest dress (which was just about as nice as the best one Pearl had) but still carried a book under her arm. I glanced at the title—*Treasure Island.*

"Ain't you read that book before?" I said.

"Yes," said Emma, "it's one of my favorites."

"What's it about?" asked Pearl.

"You wouldn't like it," I told her. "It ain't got no pictures. I checked."

"It's about a treasure map, and sailing on ships, and a pirate named Long John Silver."

"A pirate!" exclaimed Pearl.

That was all the encouragement Emma needed. By the time we'd reached the river and she'd finished telling us 'bout brave Jim Hawkins and Billy Bones and the mutiny and finding the treasure and the talking parrot, I almost felt like I'd read the book myself. And it didn't sound half bad, what with the pirates and the map and all.

"But enough about *Treasure Island*," Emma said when we reached the curve in the riverbank that made the water shallow and slow moving. "Aren't you going to teach me how to swim?"

"Gotta take off your shoes," I said.

Emma looked down at her shoes. The patent leather was dirty and scuffed already, but the leather straps were still in good shape. She glanced at the muddy water.

"But I can't see what's in the water."

"So?" I asked.

"So how will I know what's on the bottom?"

"I can tell you," chimed in Pearl. "Mud, sticks, crawdads and a rock or two."

Emma made a face.

"The normal stuff. Just be careful not to stub your toe," explained Pearl.

"Maybe I'll pass on swimming," said Emma.

"Didn't you just say you wished you could sail around the

world like one of those pirates you were telling us about?" I asked.

"Yeah."

"Well, how you gonna have an adventure like that if you're too scared to get in the river?"

Emma didn't say nothing.

"And what if you fell off the pirate ship?" asked Pearl.

"Or they made you walk the plank," I added. "Then you'd be really glad you knew how to swim."

Emma scowled. "I'm not really planning on becoming a pirate," she said. But she took her shoes and socks off just the same.

We all walked into the water till it was about up to our waists. Pearl offered Emma her hand; I expected her to refuse, but Emma clutched it like she was afraid she was gonna drift away.

"You gotta push your skirt under," said Pearl, "till it's nice and wet and stays there. Otherwise, it'll just float around you and make things harder."

"It's cold," said Emma.

"That's swimming," said Pearl.

Emma was pushing her skirt under when suddenly she screamed and lost her balance. I had to grab her arm to prevent her from falling under. "Get it off, get it off!" Emma screamed.

"What?" I asked.

She held up her foot, hopping on one leg. There was nothing on it.

"Something crawled across my toes."

Pearl nodded. "Probably a crawdad."

"What's that?" asked Emma.

"Like a little lobster. I told you about them."

Took us a while to calm Emma down, but we finally did and I showed Emma how to move her arms in the water. "Like you're digging with your hands," I explained. I tried to get her to float on her belly, and lift her head to breathe, and kick her feet too, but it was all too much.

"If I could just see what was in the water," said Emma.

"Wouldn't help you a bit," I said. "Wouldn't seeing all the fish and worms just make things worse?"

Emma didn't answer.

Finally, I gave up trying to teach Emma real swimming and Pearl just showed her how to doggy paddle. Emma kind of got that. She went in up to her neck, lifted her feet and paddled around.

It was late in the afternoon when we all walked home, letting the hot sun dry us off. "I kind of liked swimming," said Emma, which surprised me, since she'd spent most of the afternoon complaining. "Though not as much as baseball."

When we got home, Mama and Mrs. Walker were waiting on our front porch with a strange man in a suit.

"There you three are," said Mama. "We've been waiting for you." She turned to the man beside her. "This here's Mr. Rich. He's from the Rockefeller Sanitary Commission."

The man nodded politely at us. "We're trying to wipe out the hookworm infestations that are so common in rural communities."

"I don't have worms, sir," Emma said politely. "I always wear shoes."

He looked pointedly at her bare feet and the shoes in her hand.

Emma blushed and muttered, "They were teaching me to swim."

63

That's when I noticed that Mrs. Walker was holding a jar and Mama was holding two.

The man cleared his throat. "We'll just need a stool sample from everyone in town under the age of eighteen. Unless you always wear shoes. Then you couldn't have caught them."

Mama held out a jar to me and gestured toward the outhouse.

"You want me to poop here in this jar?" I asked.

Pearl giggled.

"Well, yes," said the man.

"I'd rather not," I said, and made to hand the jar back to Mama.

"Dit," Mama said sharply. "Best do as the man asks."

"Eweee!" said Pearl, but she picked up her own jar.

Emma took the jar from her mama but whispered to me before she stormed off, "If I have worms, I'm gonna kill you."

She didn't, of course. But pretty much every other kid in town did. Every evening for a week after dinner, Mama gave me and Pearl and my brothers a huge, chalky white pill. At the end of the week, I swallowed my pride along with the last pill and picked out a pair of old loafers from the barrel in the kitchen.

"Finally," Mama said with a smile. "That Emma girl's starting to rub off."

14

TRAPPING RABBITS

LATE THAT AUGUST, I CAME UP WITH A plan to make money for the Fourth hunt. I would catch rabbits and sell them to people in town. Rabbits were a cheap way of serving meat on Sunday. I figured people would pay ten to twenty cents for a big swamp rabbit.

Swamp rabbits are just like regular old cottontails 'cept they're bigger and like to swim. They have real thick, dark brown fur. Most rabbits won't go into the water 'less they're forced, but a swamp rabbit will dive under just for fun and swim along with only its little nose peeking up out of the water. The broom sage patch near the river, the one me and Emma had cut through after the buzzard, had a whole mess of rabbits, so I went down there to set up my snares.

Most people set snares that choke and kill a rabbit. Those are easy to set but make the meat tough since the rabbits tend to struggle a bit before they die. I came up with a special snare that would squeeze shut only enough to trap the rabbit, keeping it alive till you were ready to eat it. Then it was just a quick snap to break its neck and you had fresh meat for dinner.

Two days later I went back to the broom sage patch to

check my snares. No rabbits. That was unusual, but it took a couple of days for the human smell to fade from the thin wire I used. Maybe I hadn't waited long enough.

So two days later I came back again. Still no rabbits. When I looked closer, I realized all my traps had been sprung. I had caught something, but it had escaped. Wasn't even a tuft of hair left behind. That was mighty strange. I reset my snares and dreamed of huge, bald rabbits that would fetch fifty cents apiece.

When three days later I still hadn't caught nothing, I was beginning to get frustrated. Had the rabbits gone someplace else? Had I forgotten how to set a snare? Late that afternoon me and Emma were drinking root beer in our cave when I mentioned that there didn't seem to be no rabbits around this year.

"What are you talking about?" said Emma. "I've seen lots of them."

"Where?" I asked.

"Over in the broom sage patch by the river."

"What?"

"They were trapped in some old wire. I untangled them and let them go."

"You let them go?"

"Of course."

"I set those traps!"

Emma looked at me blankly. "You did?"

I nodded.

"Oh, Dit, I don't think you should do that."

"Well, it ain't up to you."

"Those poor rabbits are defenseless."

"They're food."

Emma shook her head. "I don't want you trapping them anymore."

"Those rabbits were my Fourth hunt money!" I snapped.

"The Fourth hunt is just a stupid game."

"That ain't fair, Emma." I was yelling now. "I've spent all summer showing you around Moundville. Teaching you to swim and dig a cave and throw stones and play baseball. You can't just come down here and tell me all the things we do to have fun and earn money are wrong."

"Fine," said Emma. She put down her soda and crawled out of the cave. I kicked the bottle over and watch the soda fizz out into the dirt. It didn't make me feel any better.

So I waited until I was sure she was gone, and I went down to the Black Warrior to throw some stones.

I threw stones for a long time, till my arm began to ache and I wasn't mad no more. I liked being friends with Emma. And now I'd gone and ruined it over some stupid rabbits. But the Fourth hunt wasn't stupid—not to me—so I wasn't sure what I could've done different.

I felt her come up and stand beside me. Saw her throw a couple of stones into the water until I finally turned to look at her.

"What do you want?"

"You're right," Emma said quietly.

"What?" I asked, confused.

"I'm sorry. I shouldn't tell you what to do. Mama always said I'd have more friends if I weren't so bossy."

I hadn't expected her to apologize. Chip never did that. I threw a few more stones. "You ain't so bad."

"It's just . . . I had a pet rabbit up in Boston. Used to keep her in a cage under our front porch. I had to give her away when we moved down here."

"Oh."

"I didn't have a lot of friends in Boston, Dit, even though there were tons of kids around. Sometimes, that little rabbit was the only one I could talk to."

"Oh."

"But I know people eat them down south. They served them at the potluck at our church. So I guess I can't say there's anything wrong with you trapping them."

I nodded in thanks, unsure what I was supposed to say. We threw a few more stones, then walked home without talking.

But even though Emma had given me her blessing, I felt differently about rabbits after that. Thinking about her alone, in the skinny row house, talking to her pet rabbit, well, it made me feel kind of sad. So the next day I gathered up my snares. I'd still eat rabbit stew if my mama served it, but I'd have to find another way to earn money for the Fourth hunt.

15

FRIED CHICKEN FOR SUPPER

BEFORE I KNEW IT, IT WAS THE FIRST OF
September and me and Emma were walking through the aisles
of Mrs. Pooley's store, buying pens, paper and ink for school.
Emma picked up a box of chalk and put it in her basket.

"Why you buying chalk?" I asked.

"Mama told me to get some for the teacher."

"Teacher don't need your chalk," I scoffed. "She's got
her own."

"Dit," Emma sighed. "I'm not going to your school."

Course she wasn't. There weren't no Negras at my school.
I knew that. I scuffed my shoes on the dusty floor. "Guess
you're going to the Wilson school."

"Yes, I am."

"But Elbert ain't learned nothing there. He can't read no
better than Pearl."

"Mama says I'll have to make the best of it." Emma lowered
her voice when we noticed Big Foot was standing at the end
of the aisle. "I don't really have a choice," she whispered.

Now that I thought about it, that didn't seem quite right.

Big Foot walked down the aisle toward us, a beer in one

hand. "Only one school around here for a nigger. And if you ask me, that's one too many."

I looked up at him. His mouth was drawn up in disgust, as if he had just caught me picking my nose. Emma stared at the chalk in her basket.

"Thought I told you, Dit," he continued, "stay with your own kind." He knocked me on the back of my head with the bottle and strolled over to the front counter, his dusty black boots clicking on the wooden floor.

"You won't want to be friends with me once school starts," Emma said quietly.

"Yes, I will." Sure, Emma sometimes drove me crazy with her worrying 'bout rabbits and broken windows, but spending time with her was never boring. Course school was starting soon and Chip was coming back. That got me thinking. Would he look at me the way Big Foot just did? I wondered if Emma was right.

Late that afternoon, me and Earl were helping Pa. The new corn seed had come and was doing pretty well, so now we were working on planting a late crop of turnips in Mama's garden. Mama had a big vegetable garden: tomatoes, peas, cucumbers, squash, string beans, carrots, lettuce and a whole bunch of other green leafy things I didn't much like to eat. Mama prided herself on her garden, although it seemed to me that it was us kids who did all the work. 'Cept for the canning. Mama canned so many things, we had vegetables all winter long. I wished she could be like the other mamas and run out sometime after Christmas.

To plant the turnips, Pa would dig a little hole with the hoe, then I'd drop in three tiny seeds. Earl's job was to cover them up, but he lagged a row or two behind me and Pa. The half-gallon sack of turnip seeds was heavy on my shoulder. "Pa?" I asked.

"Yes, Earl, uh, Raymond, I mean Dit?" He didn't look up.

"Why does Emma gotta go to the Wilson school? It's two miles away."

"Walking never hurt no one." My pa was big on walking.

"I know. But why don't Negras and whites go to school together?"

Pa shrugged. "Always been that way." He continued digging, each hole exactly the same.

"Don't seem fair, though." I dropped my three turnip seeds. "Specially when there's a perfectly good school just down the road."

"When I was a boy," Pa said, "the Negras ain't had no school at all."

"But after working in the fields all summer, Buster's got skin darker than Elbert," I pointed out. "And he don't go to the Wilson school."

"Skin burnt brown by the sun ain't the same thing and you know it. Besides, Elbert's light skinned 'cause his grandpa was a white man."

"His grandpa married a Negra?"

Pa stopped digging and wiped his forehead with a handkerchief. He was upset. I thought he was gonna yell at me, but all he said was: "I already said too much. Let's just concentrate on planting these turnips."

I carefully put three seeds into each hole. "I still don't understand why Emma can't go to school with me."

"Dit, just . . . gosh dang it!"

I glanced up. Earl was three or four rows behind us now. Mama's chickens were following me, eating the seeds as fast as I put them into the holes.

Pa exploded, "I'd like to kill every one of those dang birds!"

So I picked up a rock and threw it as hard as I could. It hit a chicken. The bird fell over dead. I picked up another rock, but Pa grabbed my arm. "Maybe you better not kill them all."

Pearl ran out then, her apron strings dragging on the ground. "The chickens got out! The chickens got out!"

"Thank you, Pearl," Pa said quietly. "We know."

That night, we had fried chicken for supper.

16

♡

I CALL EMMA A LIAR

THE NIGHT BEFORE THE FIRST DAY OF school, we all took a bath. Used the same tub we used for the laundry, and it took just as long to fill. For hours we boiled pots of water on the woodstove in the kitchen. We filled the tub twice, once for the boys and once for the girls. When we were all scrubbed clean, we laid out our clothes. Mama inspected them, making sure they were ironed and had no loose buttons. I had new pants, a new handkerchief and the old leather loafers from the barrel.

For breakfast Mama made sausage and eggs and grits and biscuits and let us smear butter and honey all over them. Ollie, Ulman and Elman went to the high school. Raymond, me, Earl and Pearl walked to Mrs. Seay's grammar school, two blocks away. Robert and Lois were too little for school, and they always cried on the first day 'cause they had to stay home with Mama.

I threw my book satchel over my shoulder and took off, leaving Raymond to walk with the twins. I liked to get there early and throw rocks at the two chestnut trees right next to the schoolhouse. That'd bring the chestnuts crashing down around my head. Had quite a pile collected before Mrs. Seay rang the bell and we all shuffled inside.

The schoolhouse was one room with wooden floors and a coal stove in the front for the winter. There were rows of two-person wooden desks and a big aisle down the middle of the room. Boys sat on the right and girls on the left; little kids were in the front and the older ones in the back. At the front of the room was a chalkboard and the teacher's desk.

Mrs. Seay wore a blue silk dress and her pearl necklace. A matching blue hat perched like a bird on her head. The whole outfit didn't seem too practical to me, since Mr. Summons usually ended up covered in chalk by the end of the day. But if the president of the United States stopped by and invited her to dinner, Mrs. Seay would be ready to go.

We all stood in a line in front of her, waiting to register for the year. Just ahead of me was Buster. His pa had run off a long time ago, leaving his mama with seven kids to raise alone. Even though we were the same age, his mama was so poor Buster had to work all summer in the fields. Like I'd told Pa, he was now a shade or two darker than Elbert, though his blond hair was even paler than it'd been last time I'd seen him in June. His overalls were clean, but the knees were full of holes. He didn't carry nothing, not even a pen.

"Good morning," said Mrs. Seay as she moved her ruler down her role book.

Buster swallowed hard. "Morning, ma'am."

"What's your name?"

"Buster."

"What's your real name, son?"

"Buster."

"I see." Mrs. Seay scribbled something on her list.

Buster looked at the floor. "I ain't got the tuition money yet. My mama don't get paid till next week."

"Bring it next week, then."

"Thank you, ma'am." Buster went and took a seat.

I was next in line. I held out the tuition money and smiled as she looked me over.

"You must be Harry Otis Sims," said Mrs. Seay as she took my money. She had dimples when she smiled.

"Yes, ma'am. But everybody calls me Dit."

"I hear you've got a good arm on you, Dit."

I gulped. "Uh, yes, ma'am."

She made another note in her book. "When you're playing ball at recess, please try not to break any windows." She slapped her palm with the ruler and her smile suddenly seemed a little forced. I felt my face flush and stared at my shoes.

I was so intent on getting back to my desk, I didn't see Mary's big old foot sticking out in the aisle. I tripped, dropping all my supplies. My bottle of black ink smashed on the floor, spraying me with little black dots. Everyone laughed.

I boiled with anger as I wiped up the mess with my new handkerchief. Had Emma told Mrs. Seay on me after she'd promised not to? My head started to pound. I wanted to hit someone. I might have too, 'cept Chip sat down next to me.

Chip Davidson had been my best friend since third grade. He had just gotten back from spending the summer with his grandma in Selma. Me and Chip always shared a desk at school. Chip was handsome and popular, with golden brown hair and eyes as green as emeralds. (Least that was the way my sisters described him. Tell me, which one of them had ever seen an emerald? But I guess eyes as green as pond scum just don't sound as nice.) There weren't no freckles on Chip's perfect nose, and his teeth were so white and straight, when he smiled, he fooled everyone into thinking he was a perfect angel.

They were wrong, of course. Chip's pa was the mayor of Moundville, which meant he could get away with stuff no one would put up with from anybody else. Once we accidentally set Dr. Griffith's shed on fire and I expected to end up with a whipping, but Chip talked so pretty, Mayor Davidson offered to pay for the shed and the whole incident was forgotten.

"Sure am glad to see you again, Dit," said Chip. "It was boring as sin down in Selma. My mama's so scared of the 'big city,' she barely let me out the front door."

"So what'd you do all day?" I asked, happy to think of something besides the little black stains on my new pants.

"Played dominoes with my cousins."

"That's it?"

"Well, once my older cousin snuck me into the pool hall. But my grandma caught us 'fore we could finish even one game."

"Too bad." Wasn't sure I believed him about the pool hall. Chip's been known to exaggerate.

"So what about you, Dit?" asked Chip. "Heard a family of Negras moved in next door."

I shrugged. "It ain't so bad."

"Course Dit don't think it's bad," said Buster, sitting alone behind us. "He's in love with their girl!"

"No, I ain't!"

"My brother says you always running around with her," Buster said.

"No," I lied.

Chip grinned. "Dit's got a girlfriend!"

"Shut up." I tried to ignore them, but they kept chanting, "Girlfriend, girlfriend."

For the first time ever, I was glad when the teacher stood up and made us start learning.

After school, me and Chip walked home, talking about baseball and laughing. I didn't even notice Emma till she ran right up to me. "Hi, Dit," she said all out of breath. "You won't believe what happened to me today."

Chip took a long look at Emma, and poked me in the ribs.

"The teacher made a mistake in a long division problem," Emma continued. "I pointed it out and instead of thanking me, she scolded me for speaking out of turn! I think you're right, Dit. I don't think I'm going to like that Wilson school."

I didn't say nothing. Chip snickered and made kissing sounds. I jabbed him with my elbow and he shut up.

Emma looked at Chip, then back at me. "Is something wrong?"

"You told Mrs. Seay I threw stones at her house!" Soon as I said it, I felt like a fool. I hadn't meant to just accuse her. All afternoon I'd been telling myself, talk to her softly, sometime when you're alone. But then when she embarrassed me by being my friend in front of Chip, it just came bursting out.

"You threw stones at Mrs. Seay's house?" Chip asked.

"I didn't tell," Emma stated firmly.

I snorted. "Mrs. Seay said to me, 'Be sure not to break no more windows.' How else would she know?"

"It wasn't me," Emma protested. "You know I promised not to."

"Your promise ain't worth a dang!" Then I spit in the dirt.

Emma's face swelled up like an insect bite. I thought for

sure she was gonna burst into tears, but she just picked up her skirt and ran off in the opposite direction.

Me and Chip watched her go. "You threw stones at Mrs. Seay's house?" he asked again.

"Yeah," I admitted.

"And the nigger girl knew about it?"

I just kicked at the dirt. Chip knew I hung out with Elbert during the summer, and he had never called him a nigger. I wanted to tell him not to call Emma that, but the words just wouldn't come out.

"I gotta go home now," I said.

Chip nodded. He knew I had chores after school, and I knew he didn't.

"See you tomorrow," I said, and ran off.

That evening as we were getting ready for bed, I told Raymond what had happened. He just shook his head. "Well, shoot, Dit, everyone knows you've got the best arm in town. And you did break Dr. Griffith's window last year playing ball. Word gets around."

He was right. People had teased me for months about that. I had forgotten. "Maybe Emma didn't tell," said Raymond.

I had a sinking feeling he was right.

17

FUN AND GAMES

THE MORE I THOUGHT ABOUT IT, THE SURER
I was that Emma hadn't told. Who would she have blabbed my
secret to? I didn't think she had any other friends. But I didn't
do nothing about it, not even when I saw Emma on the way to
school the next morning. I wanted to call out to her, but before
I could think of what to say, she turned on her heel and ran
away, fast as a spooked rabbit.

I trudged into school and sat down next to Chip. When
Mrs. Seay was busy up front helping the little kids with their
reading, I turned to him and said, "I ain't seeing that Negra girl
no more."

"Course you ain't," said Chip, pretending to work on his
arithmetic assignment. "Cause you got your eyes closed when
you're kissing her."

Behind us, Buster snorted and chuckled.

"I'm serious, Chip."

"I know. Kissing is serious business."

Buster just laughed harder.

I turned to look at Buster. "What's so funny?"

"You are," said Buster.

"Shut up!"

Mrs. Seay looked up then. "There's a lot of talking going on." She looked around the room and caught my eye. "Dit, stand up, please."

I scrambled to my feet.

"Is there something wrong?" Mrs. Seay asked.

"No, ma'am." I looked her straight in the eye, feeling my face burning up like a kettle left on a stove after it's boiled dry.

"Good. Please get back to your arithmetic."

"Yes, ma'am." I sat back down and looked at my math book. Chip had drawn little hearts over half the problems so I couldn't read the numbers.

"Chip!" I hissed.

"Just tell Mrs. Seay you couldn't do your work 'cause you were blinded by love."

"I ain't in love!"

"That's what my brother said," chimed in Buster. "Right before he got married."

They burst into laughter. Mrs. Seay turned around and glared but didn't say nothing to them. I ground my teeth and pretended to concentrate on my work.

At recess, things just got worse. Chip and Buster wanted to play marbles, so I drew a big circle in the dirt. We put our marbles in the middle, then took turns flicking our shooters into the circle. If your shooter pushes another marble out of the circle, you get to keep that marble and go again. The person who ends up with the most marbles wins.

Everything was okay at first, till I won the first game. We ain't supposed to gamble at school, but we had each bet a nickel. This meant I had won ten cents. Chip smiled and said, "Now you can buy something for your sweetie."

"Dit's got a sweetheart! Dit's got a sweetheart!" chanted Buster.

"Hush up, Buster," I said. "Let's just play another game."

So we did. But every time my shooter hit a marble out of the circle, Chip puckered up his lips and made kissing noises.

"That's seventeen kisses!" Buster exclaimed.

"Come on, stop it." This just made the guys laugh harder. I glanced over, looking for my brothers. Raymond and Earl were way off over by a tree playing catch. Pearl was watching the marble game, but I couldn't exactly ask her for help without making things even worse. So I figured I'd just have to join in.

"Fine, I admit it." I threw my hands up in the air. "I sure do love that Negra. Watch out, Emma, here's kiss number eighteen!"

The boys roared with laughter.

I flicked my shooter and knocked two more of their marbles out of the circle. "Nineteen and twenty. My, those kisses are fine!" I cried, loud as can be.

Buster was laughing so hard he started to hiccup.

"How about a hug now?" I went on. "Smooch, smooch, smooch!"

Chip had tears in his eyes. "Oh, Dit," Chip cried. "You are just too funny!"

But when I glanced over at Pearl, she wasn't laughing.

On the way home, it seemed the Emma joke had finally grown stale. Me and Buster didn't have much to say, so Chip turned his attention to Pearl's best friend, Mary. Mary was a sweet girl, though not the quickest in school. She was especially bad at spelling. Mary and Pearl were just ahead of us when Chip started in. "That was sure a fun spelling bee this afternoon."

"Sure was," Buster said.

"Whole bunch of easy words. Like *bake*," said Chip.

Course that was one of the words Mary had gotten wrong.

"And *why*," added Buster.

Mary had spelled it *w-h-i-y*.

Pearl turned around to look at me. I just shook my head. She put her arm around Mary, and the two girls started to walk faster.

"Though there were some hard words too," said Chip. "Like *Mary*."

I knew where this was going. The old postmaster had a girl named Isabelle. She'd needed glasses but her daddy'd been too cheap to spend the money, so she'd squinted all the time. We had played the same joke on her.

"I know how to spell *Mary*," Buster said. "*S-t-u-p-i-d.*"

Pearl looked at me again. I had to say something. Mary was staring at the ground.

"Knock it off, Buster," I said.

They ignored me.

"*Mary?*" said Chip. "I thought it was *d-u-m-b.*"

"You're gonna make her cry," I warned.

Sure enough, soon as I said it, Mary started crying.

"Now look what you did, Dit!" scolded Chip. "Shame on you."

"Me! It was you."

Chip shrugged. "It's just fun and games." He pointed to Mary. "Even Mary knows that."

Mary nodded, even as she kept crying. Pearl sat down with her by the side of the road as me, Chip and Buster walked on by.

It had been my idea last year to spell Isabelle *i-d-i-o-t*. I remembered laughing as she cried. But this year it didn't seem funny. And I finally realized that the idiot had been me.

18

THE DONKEY

THAT EVENING I SAT AT THE DINING ROOM table doing my homework with Pearl and Earl. The light from our oil lamp was dim, and the numbers seemed to swim in front of my eyes. "Mama?" I finally called out.

Mama walked into the dining room, Lois crying on her hip. "What, Dit?"

"I don't understand this." I pointed to my math homework.

"Well, I can't help you now." Mama sounded tired. "I gotta get the little ones to bed."

"But Mama . . ."

"Just do your best." She walked out of the room. Mama was still mad at me for getting ink on my new clothes on the very first day of school.

I stared at my paper and finally realized what was bugging me: I had made things right with Chip, but not with Emma. I slid off my chair and headed toward the door.

"Where you going?" asked Pearl.

"Out."

"I'm gonna tell!"

I let the screen door slam behind me.

A moment later, I stood on Emma's front porch, still clutching my book and papers. Must have raised my hand three times before I finally got up the nerve to knock. After a minute or two, Mrs. Walker came to the front door. She didn't say nothing.

"May I speak to Emma, please?" I asked, looking at the wide, clean-swept boards that made up her front porch.

"She doesn't want to see you," Mrs. Walker said. She had a clean apron on over her work dress and smelled like baking bread.

"I know, ma'am." I forced myself to look her in the eye. "That's why I gotta talk to her."

Mrs. Walker nodded and led me into the parlor. Emma was sitting on the couch reading a book—*Tarzan of the Apes*. What the heck kind of name was Tarzan?

Emma put down her book and folded her hands in her lap as I approached.

I took a deep breath. "I shouldn't have accused you of telling." It was hard, but once I started, the words came a little easier. "You gave me your word, and I know you ain't gonna break it."

"You hurt my feelings," Emma said.

"I'm sorry."

There was a long pause.

"I ain't never apologized to no one before," I said finally. "Am I doing it right?"

Emma gave a little smile. "Mama just made biscuits," she said. "Would you like one?"

"Sure." The biscuits were delicious. I thought admitting I

was wrong would cause me to pop like a balloon. Instead, I felt like a donkey had been sitting on my chest and I'd finally convinced him to stand up.

While we ate, Emma told me about Tarzan. She went on and on for the time it took me to eat three biscuits, but I still wasn't sure I understood the story.

"So there's this boy, Tarzan," I repeated. "And when his parents die, he's raised by an ape mama?"

Emma nodded. "Her name's Kala."

"And he teaches himself to read with an old primer?" I asked.

"Yes," Emma explained. "And then another man teaches him to speak French and . . ."

"Do the apes speak French?"

"No, but . . ."

I shook my head. "That story sounds a bit too complicated for me. Anyway, I gotta get on home. Maybe Mama finally has time to help me with my long division."

"I can help you with that," said Emma.

"You can?" I asked.

Before I could say anything else, Emma had shown me how to divide 4,673 by 22, explained how to bring down the numbers and write the remainder at the top. Didn't take but five minutes, and Emma smiled when we were done. "You catch on quick, Dit."

"Nah," I said. "I ain't good at math."

"Who told you that?" she asked.

I shrugged.

Afterward, as I was walking out the door, I heard Mrs. Walker say to Mr. Walker, "I've never heard a white boy apologize to my girl before," and I could hear the smile in her voice.

19

THE PLANE

EVERY DAY AFTER SCHOOL, I'D HURRY through my chores and head over to the mounds to meet Emma in our cave. We'd skip stones, or practice throwing baseballs, or collect acorns, or just sit and talk. Sometimes, she'd paint my picture as I lay on the riverbank and looked at the sky. My skin would get all prickly when I felt her squinting at me in the sunlight. Looking at her pictures was strange: they were me, but something was always different. My hair was the wrong shade of red or my ears were too big. When I complained to Emma, she just laughed.

But I didn't talk about Emma at school, and Chip didn't ask. I wanted to be Chip's friend too. If he liked me, everyone at school liked me. We talked baseball and played marbles at recess, and if it wasn't as much fun as I'd remembered, that didn't have nothing to do with Emma. How could it? She wasn't even there.

'Cept sometimes it was like she was there, 'cause I could hear her asking me all sorts of questions. Why hadn't I ever noticed that Chip's teasing sometimes made the little kids cry? Why did I sometimes join in the teasing? Why did Chip suddenly want to spend more time with Buster? Why did Buster say yes to everything Chip wanted to do? Why did Chip and Buster play with Elbert on the ball field but wouldn't speak to him if they ran into him on Mrs. Pooley's front porch? Why did Chip cheat at marbles? Why'd I cheat at marbles? Why was it okay to like girls when you were a little kid, bad when you were a big kid and then okay to marry them once you were all grown up? And why, if Chip was my real good friend, was I so scared to mention Emma?

Things went along like this for a month or so, with me wondering and why-ing till my head felt like it was screwed on backwards. Got so I didn't say much around Chip and Buster 'cause I was so worried one of those "Emma questions" would come bursting out. I had my school friends and my after-school friends. Oh, they knew about each other—Moundville ain't that big and people talk—but Chip and Buster had tired of teasing me. Least it seemed that way, till the first week in October.

Mrs. Seay liked to call people up to the chalkboard to do math problems. Kept her from getting her hands all covered in chalk. Mary was standing in front of the whole class, scratching her head. "My problem was 67 times 43. I got 469," she said, shuffling her feet. "But I don't think that's right."

Mrs. Seay shook her head. "Can anyone help Mary?"

I raised my hand. "You forgot to bring down the zero," I said, remembering what Emma had told me.

Mrs. Seay nodded. Chip and Buster laughed at Mary as she sat down, but not me. I had gotten the same problem wrong the night before.

Mrs. Seay asked Raymond to come to the board next. He

was in the middle of his problem when a soft buzzing started. It quickly turned into a loud roar, a roar I couldn't forget, specially since I'd once mistaken it for a buzzard.

"It's a plane!" I said.

Everyone jumped out of their seats and ran to the window.

"Students, please!" Mrs. Seay cried. "I know you've probably never seen a plane before, but . . ." No one was listening to her, so Mrs. Seay finally gave up and hurried over to the window herself.

The plane was circling, and with each circle it came closer to the ground. "Is he landing?" asked Raymond.

I couldn't wait no longer. I jumped out of the window and raced toward the empty lot where we played baseball. If a pilot were gonna land, that'd be the best place in town.

Chip, Raymond and Pearl were at my heels. "It's down there, behind those trees," Chip called out.

We pushed through the row of trees and onto the empty lot, but there was nothing there.

"Did he crash?" asked Pearl. We all stood still, gasping for breath.

Uncle Wiggens hobbled onto the field. "Jesus, Joseph and General Lee." He stood huffing for a moment. "Big Foot said the pilot landed in the big field out past the railroad yard." That was over near the Wilson school. We took off at a run.

Seemed like forever till we burst out of the forest and found the plane sitting in a cow pasture. The cows were annoyed. They mooed loudly at the big, silver machine that had interrupted their grazing. Most of the town was there too: Doc Haley, Mayor Davidson, Mrs. Pooley, Big Foot, Pa and Mama, Emma's parents, Dr. Griffith, Emma, Elbert and a bunch of the other kids from the Wilson school. We were all staring at the plane.

The pilot stood on the ground, leaning against one wing. He was a young man, with sweaty brown hair that stuck to his forehead, and held a helmet under one arm. Mayor Davidson walked over to greet him. "Welcome to Moundville."

The pilot took Mayor Davidson's hand and shook it heartily. "Thank you, sir." Then he turned to the crowd. "Sorry to cause all this commotion, folks. I'm afraid I ran out of gas." Everyone laughed. The young man grinned. "Could somebody fetch me a few gallons?"

Two older boys took off at a run before I could even think about moving. Emma pushed her way through the crowd to me. "Did you see it, Dit?" she cried. "Did you see it land?"

I shook my head. "I just got here."

"It was beautiful!" Emma continued. "Just glided in like an eagle."

I glanced over at Chip and Buster and saw them watching me and Emma talking. They started laughing, and even though I was too far away to hear their words, I knew what they were saying.

Emma saw them too. "Something wrong, Dit?"

I shook my head again.

Mrs. Seay eventually arrived to tell us that school had been dismissed for the day. Her hat had blown off her head, and her pale cheeks were rosy with excitement. When the boys came back with the gas, me and Emma pushed our way to the front of the crowd. We stood beside the wings of the plane, stroking the shiny metal.

I saw Elbert across the way and waved. He waved back till

he saw Emma standing next to me. Then he frowned and turned away.

Before I could decide what to make of that, the pilot jumped onto the wing. He stood up, balanced himself with outstretched arms and poured the gasoline into a hidden tank. When he was finished, he jumped down right next to me and Emma.

"You like planes?" he asked.

"Yes, sir," Emma answered.

"Maybe you'll get to take a ride someday."

Emma's eyes shone. "I sure hope so."

The pilot winked at us, then Big Foot and Dr. Griffith forced all the children back.

"Hold her tight," the pilot instructed the grown-ups, "till I'm ready to go."

Big Foot, Dr. Griffith, Mr. Walker and Pa held on to the wings of the plane. The pilot spun the propeller and the engine sprang to life with a mighty roar.

The pilot climbed back into the cockpit, adjusted his controls and gave a thumbs-up. The men let go and scattered. The plane shot forward, slowly lifting off the ground.

It headed straight for a grove of trees.

"He's not gonna make it!" Mrs. Pooley cried. She covered her eyes.

But at the last moment, the plane rose up and just brushed the top of the branches.

"What a relief!" Mrs. Seay sighed. "I was afraid he was going to crash."

But as I walked home, I didn't feel relieved. I felt worried. Worried that the days of keeping my friends separate were just about over.

20

STRIKING OUT

THE DAY AFTER THE PLANE CAME TO town, I convinced Emma to give baseball another try. I sent her way out in right field, and for the first two innings not a ball came near her. Then Elman hit a ground ball and Emma actually managed to pick it up and throw it to first. She grinned like a horse with a mouthful of sugar. Of course, by that point Elman had already made it to third, but it was a start.

By the time she got up to bat, however, Emma was no longer smiling.

"You okay, Emma?" I asked.

"Dit, I can't do this." Her hands trembled.

"Sure you can," I said as I handed her a bat and pushed her toward home plate. "It's easy," I said, though she was holding the bat all wrong.

Raymond threw the first pitch. It was a nice, slow ball. Emma winced and jumped to one side.

"Strike one," cried Buster. He was catching, and Chip was on first. They hadn't made no kissing noises or girlfriend jokes at school that day. Maybe I'd been wrong about them whispering about me and Emma when the plane landed.

Raymond threw the next pitch. It was nice and easy again. Emma swung, missing the ball by a mile.

"Strike two!" Buster sounded pleased.

"Emma," Raymond yelled. "I'm trying to make it easy for you!"

Emma bit her lip. Raymond pitched again. Any gentler and the ball would have dropped out of the air. Emma swung so hard, she fell to the ground.

"Strike three. You're out!" Buster yelled.

Emma left the bat on the ground and walked back to the circle of old stumps we used as our dugout.

"Don't worry, Emma," Pearl said before taking her turn at bat. "Nobody hits the ball every time."

Emma started to cry.

"You'll hit it next time," I said without much conviction, watching the tears drip off her chin onto the dusty ground.

"Next time," Emma spat, wiping her nose. "There's not going to be a next time."

There was a loud crack. We looked over. Pearl was sliding into first base.

"Even Pearl can do it," Emma moaned. "Why do you think I'm so good at reading? It's because I can't do anything else!"

She was probably right, but I didn't think it would make her feel better to hear me say it. I stood watching her cry, unsure what to do.

Mitch, the slow boy, lumbered over to her and put his arm around her. "Don't cry, little Emma," he said as if talking to a puppy. "I ain't no good at reading."

Emma hiccuped and gave a little giggle. Mitch's face broke into its usual grin. I felt all churned up inside, like milk before it turns to butter. Mitch had found a way to comfort Emma, while I just stood there like a fool.

I was up to bat next. Raymond was a decent pitcher, but I could usually get a single or maybe even a double off of him. He threw a fastball, but I knew I could hit it, so I started to swing.

"Girlfriend," muttered Buster, just loud enough for me to hear.

I was thrown off balance and the ball snapped into his glove. In a loud voice he called, "Strike one."

The next pitch was a curveball. Soon as I swung again, Buster whispered, "Saw you with her."

Strike two.

I turned to face him this time. "What'd you say?"

"Nothing."

Buster exchanged a glance with Chip on first, and I knew it wasn't just about baseball. But I didn't know what to do. Raymond was waiting and everyone was watching me, so finally, I just stepped back up to home plate.

Raymond threw the ball.

Buster hissed, "Nigger lover," but this time, I hit the ball. Might even have been a triple, but instead of running, I threw down my bat.

"Say it again," I yelled. "Say it to my face!"

"Say what?" said Buster with a smirk.

I slugged him. Hit him right in his nose. He staggered but didn't fall over, so I punched him in the stomach. He jumped me then, and even though we were the same size, he was stronger from working all summer. It might have gone pretty bad for me, 'cept the one good thing about having so many brothers and sisters is there's always someone to pull you out of a fight.

Before I knew what was happening, Raymond and Elman were holding me and Chip had Buster. Blood was running down Buster's nose, and I knew I'd have a black eye. Emma had disappeared and Pearl was crying and I didn't know if I was mad at Buster or Chip or Mitch or Emma or even myself. I only knew that even though I had hit the ball, I had most definitely struck out.

21

THE SECRET

THE NEXT DAY AT SCHOOL CHIP ASKED Mrs. Seay if he could switch desks and go sit with Buster. Mrs. Seay gave me a funny look, but I didn't say nothing and Buster didn't have a desk partner, so finally she nodded. Chip didn't look at me as he walked back to our desk and collected his things. We'd sat together since third grade.

The rest of the day, I could see Mrs. Seay talking, but I couldn't hear nothing. The empty space beside me was like a whirlpool, sucking away all my thoughts, getting louder and louder, till all I could hear was its roar.

After school, I rushed through my chores. I didn't dare show my face at the baseball game, and I wasn't ready to face Emma, so I decided to pay Elbert a visit. I was gonna put my problems at school out of my mind and focus on the Fourth hunt. Since my plan with the rabbits hadn't worked out too well, I was gonna collect me some scrap metal. With the war going on, Ulman said if you were willing to put in the time collecting old bottle caps and wire, you could be rich. Maybe I could convince Elbert to ditch the store for an afternoon and help me out.

But Elbert wasn't too enthusiastic when I ran the idea by him. "Haven't seen you around much, Dit," he said as he swept off the porch outside of the barbershop.

"I've been busy." Felt a little bad about that. Even if Elbert couldn't go fishing as much as he'd used to, I could've stopped by just to say hello. Afraid I couldn't remember the last time I'd done that.

"Busy with that Emma girl?" He didn't look up from his sweeping.

"She's all right, Elbert."

"What happened to your eye?"

I was annoyed 'cause I knew he'd heard about it. "Got in a fight. Why weren't you at the game anyway?"

"Don't have time for games. You know I've been helping out my pa. Getting pretty good at cutting hair too."

Took a long look at Elbert then. He was only fifteen, but suddenly he seemed a lot older. He was taller, his shoulders were broader and I'll be a monkey's uncle if there wasn't fuzz on his upper lip and chin. Elbert had gone and grown himself a beard!

"You aren't sweet on her, are you?" he asked.

"What?" Elbert had been talking, but I guess the whirlpool was still roaring in my head, 'cause I hadn't heard a word.

"Emma," he repeated. "You ain't sweet on her?"

"No."

"Good. Whites and Negras shouldn't be sweet on each other," Elbert said firmly.

"I thought your grandpa was a white man?" I asked.

Elbert froze like he'd just spied a copperhead, about to strike. "Who told you that?" he whispered.

"My pa."

Elbert took a step closer. His mouth screwed up like he'd bit into an old lemon. "I ain't supposed to talk about it."

"Come on, Elbert."

He rolled the broom handle back and forth in his hands. "My grandpa was a white man, a big plantation owner. Took my grandma out in the woods and nine months later she had my pa."

"Without being married or nothing?" I said. My voice sounded too loud.

Elbert shook his head. "And guess who the man was."

"Who?"

"You can't tell no one."

"I won't."

Elbert took a deep breath, then lowered his voice till I could barely hear him. "Big Foot's daddy."

"Big Foot's your uncle?"

"Shhh!" Elbert glanced around, though we were alone on the street. "You can't tell no one or there'll be trouble."

"I promise."

We were both quiet for a while, then Elbert asked, "So you sure you ain't sweet on that Emma?"

"She ain't my girlfriend," I said firmly. Then an awful thought occurred to me. "Are you sweet on her?"

"No," said Elbert.

"Good." I felt more relieved than I expected. Finally I blurted out, "You gonna help me get rich or not?"

Elbert sighed. "My pa is over at the church. Really should ask him if . . ."

"Aw, shoot, Elbert. You know he'll be busy there all afternoon."

Elbert smiled then, the old familiar smile I remembered. "Sure," he said. "Give me a minute to close up and then let's go find us some scrap metal."

22

THE BUZZARD,
PART 2

NEXT DAY AFTER SCHOOL, DOC HALEY was back at the shop and Elbert was busy giving Reverend Cannon a shave and shoe shine, so I went off to collect some scrap metal by myself. While I was pulling some wire out of a tree, I stumbled onto an old nest. In the nest were some owl pellets. I broke them apart with a stick and poked at the skeletons of mice the owl had swallowed whole, digested and then spit back up.

That got me thinking 'bout the buzzard I had killed way back in July. It was now the middle of October. The bird was probably just a skeleton and feathers, but I had avoided that path all autumn, so I hadn't seen it. I decided to go and take a look.

But Emma wasn't interested in coming with me. "I don't want to see it," she said, and put her nose back in the book she was reading. It said *The Secret Garden* on the front.

"You scared?" I taunted.

She rocked in her chair without answering.

I hadn't seen Emma since I beat up Buster. "Come on," I coaxed. "We'll just take a quick look at the buzzard."

"Why?"

I didn't want to go see the buzzard alone. But I didn't want to admit that, so I just said, "Buzzards eat dead animals. I want to see if its friends ate it up."

"Yuck," said Emma.

"And I can practice shooting some squirrels."

"Why do you have to kill anything?"

"I already told you, hunting ain't killing. And I gotta practice for the Fourth hunt."

Emma went back to reading. I knew how she felt about the Fourth hunt. If I wanted her to come with me, I needed to come up with something else.

"That a good book?" I asked.

"Yes."

I knew Emma loved to talk about the books she was reading, and she was a pretty good storyteller. It started when Pearl had asked her about *Treasure Island* in the summer. Then there was the time she'd helped me with my math and told me all about *Tarzan*. Maybe the garden book was more interesting than it sounded too. "Come look at the buzzard with me, I'll let you tell me about that old secret garden on the way home."

Emma closed her book with a snap. "Fine," she grumbled. "Let's go."

I grabbed my shotgun and we started off down the path by the river. The leaves were changing color, and some even had already fallen off the trees. They crunched under our feet. The sun shone through the half-bare branches, Emma was collecting all the leaves that were red like my hair and we were having such a good time, I just about forgot where we were going. Emma was the one who stopped suddenly and pointed to the large pile of feathers on the ground just ahead of us.

I picked up a stick and walked toward it. It was bigger than I remembered. I poked the pile.

The buzzard jumped up.

I was so surprised I stumbled back a few feet and fell down in the dirt.

The buzzard wasn't dead. Looked even more awful than a normal buzzard, with skin stretched tight across its skeleton. Half of its dirty, rotten feathers had fallen out. It was flapping its left wing and snapping wildly with its beak. Before I could move, it took a big chunk of leather out of my shoe and a bite of my big toe as well.

"Ahhh!" I screamed. Blood started to ooze from the hole in my shoe.

I scrambled to my feet and hobbled away. My heart was pounding. "How come it's still alive?" I asked.

"You must have broken its wing," said Emma. "It probably can go a while without food."

Buzzard don't eat too regular, it's true. But it hadn't been a couple of weeks—it had been three months.

I watched the buzzard hopping around in front of me. Its right wing had healed at an odd angle; the bird would never fly again. It ran in crazed circles.

"He's starving to death," said Emma.

Then I knew what I had to do, but I just couldn't make myself pick up that gun. How could I feel so sick about killing something I had thought was already dead? "What if I brought it food every couple of weeks, maybe a fish or an old chicken leg?"

"Dit," said Emma softly, "you have to shoot it."

And I knew she was right. I lifted the shotgun to my shoulder. My foot throbbed and it was hard to balance. The buzzard stopped running then and raised its head, like it wanted to be sure I had a clear shot. I fired and the bird stopped moving.

Finally had a chance to sit down and tend to my foot. Emma gave me her handkerchief and I pressed it against my toe to stop the bleeding.

"We should bury it," said Emma, looking at the lump of bones and feathers.

"No," I said quietly. "The other buzzards will be circling soon. At least they can have a decent meal."

Emma let me lean on her shoulder as I limped back down the path, dragging the gun behind me. The leaves crunched underfoot, just like they had done before, but the color seemed to have drained out of the day. I couldn't think of nothing to say.

"Shooting that buzzard was wrong," Emma said finally.

"You told me to," I protested.

"I mean the first time, not the second."

I thought about it for a moment. If I had extra dead squirrels, I could throw them to the dogs. They had to eat too. But even our old mutt wouldn't touch a dead buzzard, so there was no reason to kill one. "I know," I said softly. "I won't do it again."

"You promise?" asked Emma.

"I promise," I said. "I won't kill any more animals."

"Good," said Emma.

"Least not for fun, anyway."

Emma muttered something under her breath, but I didn't quite hear her.

We stumbled on a few more yards. "I probably shouldn't have beat up Buster either."

"Probably not," said Emma, helping me over an old log that lay across the path.

"But he deserved it. Way more than the buzzard!"

She smiled, then seemed to think better of it. "What did he say?" Emma asked.

"Who?"

"Buster. I saw him whisper to you, right before you hit him."

I told her. Didn't want to, but she had asked.

Her face got real still. I swear she didn't even blink for over a minute. Then she shook her head. "You don't have to defend me, Dit."

"Yes, I do," I said. "You're my friend."

She was silent for a long time. Finally, she said, "I've never had a friend like you."

I thought that was a compliment, but I wasn't quite sure. We walked without talking a little bit longer. The afternoon air was warm and everything was still. It seemed like we were the only two people in the forest.

"You ain't gonna tell no one 'bout the buzzard, are you?" I asked.

"Teach me how to hit a baseball," she said, "and I'll keep your secret."

"I already taught you to throw a ball," I grumbled.

"Throwing a ball without being able to hit it doesn't do me much good."

She had a point. "Then you gotta help me with my school-work," I said.

"I already do that."

She had a point there too. "Well, you gotta keep doing it," I insisted.

"Sure." And when she smiled again, I hardly felt my toe ache.

But my brain kept right on doing somersaults. I thought about how I was wrong to shoot the buzzard the first time but right to put it out of its suffering the second. Thought about wings healing crooked and longing to jump in the air and fly but being forced to scuttle about on the ground. Thought about how I suddenly wasn't sorry for beating up Buster, even if it meant I had to sit alone at school. And I realized that when I spent time with Chip and Buster, I didn't do much thinking at all.

23

EASY AS BREATHING

WE WENT BACK TO EMMA'S HOUSE AND told her mama that I had slipped on some rocks and stubbed my toe. Mrs. Walker had worked as a practical nurse in Boston, and she'd started giving out teas and salves in Moundville too. People said she had magic in her fingers. It was true—a cut she dressed healed twice as fast as normal. I'd have thought Dr. Griffith would've been jealous, but he seemed to like Mrs. Walker. Sometimes they even traded remedies for ringworm or whooping cough.

Mrs. Walker clucked over me for a while and made me wash my foot with soap and water. "That's the strangest-looking stubbed toe I've ever seen," she said, but I guess she bought our story, 'cause she didn't ask any more questions. Just put some iodine on my wound, gave us some milk and biscuits and left us alone.

I collected my mitt, an old bat and my twine baseball and led Emma back into the woods. We picked a small clearing in the shadow of a mound and I handed her the bat.

To me, baseball was as easy as breathing, but Emma didn't even know how to hold the bat. I had to think real hard before

I could explain it to her. "Hold your hands closer together," I told her finally. "And bend your knees."

When Emma was holding the bat in a way that didn't look too awful, I took a couple of steps back, picked up the twine ball and threw it toward her. She panicked, swung way too soon and stepped right into the path of the ball. It hit her in the side with a loud thump. Tears welled up in her eyes and she sat down on the ground.

Our lesson was over.

The next day after school, we tried again. Emma flinched and ran anytime I threw the ball anywhere near her. "What's wrong?" I asked. "Are you scared of the ball?"

"Yes," Emma answered, and pulled up her shirt. She had a huge bruise on her ribs from the day before.

"You can't play baseball if you're scared," I pointed out. "Guess I'm gonna have to teach you how to watch the ball."

"I know how to watch the ball," Emma said.

"No, you don't. You got to be able to sense where the ball is," I explained. "And if you can do that, you won't get hit."

"How are you going to teach me that?" asked Emma.

I thought for a moment. "All you have to do is stand still. I'm gonna throw the ball to one side of you or the other. You yell 'left' or 'right' depending on which side the ball passes."

"I don't need any more bruises."

"I ain't gonna hit you, Emma."

"You promise?"

"I promise. Don't you trust me?"

Emma nodded.

"All right, then. Let's play ball."

At first, Emma just stood there looking confused. I kept throwing. Right, left, left, left, right. Then, when she finally started believing I wasn't gonna hit her, she guessed, calling out "right" and "left" more or less at random. Pretty soon, she was getting more right than wrong. A couple of days later, we moved on to picking up the bat.

About the time Emma's bruise began to fade, Mrs. Seay decided we should learn the capitals of all forty-eight states. Instead of half paying attention, I forced myself to copy them carefully into my notebook. Then I asked Emma for help. She suggested we combine our projects.

I'd step up to the mound and Emma would ask, "Pennsylvania?"

"Harrisburg," I'd answer, then throw the ball. She'd swing and miss.

"New York?" she asked.

"Albany," I answered. I pitched. She swung and missed.

"Massachusetts?"

"Boston."

Emma smiled. And 'cause she was smiling, she forgot to think. I pitched, she swung and we both jumped at the crack when the bat connected with the ball.

24

I MAKE DOC HALEY
REAL, REAL MAD

THE NEXT AFTERNOON WE TOOK A BREAK
from baseball so I could get my hair cut by Doc Haley. I was
supposed to sing in the church choir on Sunday and Mama
wanted me to look nice. Elbert came out of the back room and
asked me if I wanted to go fishing when I was done. "Sure," I
said. "Why don't you swing by Emma's and see if she wants to
go too?"

"Never mind," he said. "Got some chores I should take care
of." He let the door slam on his way out.

Doc Haley looked up when the bells jangled, but he didn't
say nothing.

"You think it's a bad thing I'm friends with Emma?" I
asked.

Doc snipped at a piece of my hair. "It ain't bad," he said
slowly.

"Elbert don't like her much," I said. "I don't think you do
neither."

He shook his head. "I like Emma just fine. It's just . . ." Doc
shrugged. "No good's ever come of a white boy hanging around
a Negra girl."

"You talking about Elbert's grandpa?" I asked.

Doc froze, just as Elbert had done, and I remembered I'd promised not to say nothing. But surely Doc knew 'bout his own daddy.

"Where'd you hear about that?" he asked, his voice serious and cold.

Before I could think up a good lie, the front door jingled and Big Foot stepped into the store. Doc put down his scissors and wiped his hands on his white apron. "Afternoon, Mr. Big Foot, sir. What can I do for you today? Shoe shine?"

Big Foot headed straight to the shelf, picked up a bottle of hair tonic and put it in his pocket. Then he walked back to the door.

"Big Foot?" I called out from the chair.

He paused in the doorway. "What, Dit?"

"You forgot to pay for that," I said.

Big Foot's cheeks turned as red as his nose, and I noticed a fine white scar down the left side of his face. He was completely clean shaven except for a few bristles sprouting out on each side of that scar.

"No, sir," said Doc quickly. "The boy's mistaken. That tonic's a gift to you."

Big Foot grunted and fished a quarter out of his pocket. He threw it into a bowl on Doc Haley's counter. "You mind your own business, Dit," he growled, and strolled out of the store.

Doc Haley snatched the towel from my neck and shook it out, even though he wasn't finished with my haircut. Little flecks of my red hair stuck to the tile floor like bits of dried blood.

"What the heck you think you're doing?" he asked in an angry whisper.

"He was trying to steal from you."

"He's stole from me for twenty years," Doc snapped. "It's no concern of yours."

"I'm sorry."

"You be careful, Dit. Big Foot killed a man in Selma."

"Really?"

"In a bar fight. Claimed it was an accident, but everyone knew it wasn't." Doc Haley glared at me. A vein was pulsing on the side of his head. I ain't never seen him so angry.

"I said I was sorry."

"Sorry don't help, Dit, if somebody ends up dead." He took one of the towels he used for giving shaves, soaked it in a bowl of cool water and pressed it to his temples. "You'd best get along home now."

I slid slowly off the big chair. On the way home, I thought about what Doc had said about Big Foot. The sheriff did have a temper. He had fists the size of Mama's apple pie pans. And the scar on his cheek I had never noticed before. I supposed it was possible that Big Foot had killed a man. And I wasn't sure if I should be impressed or scared.

25

KITTENS

SINCE I WAS SPENDING MOST OF MY TIME helping Emma with baseball, I wasn't making much money collecting scrap metal. Besides, the iron dealer was a cheat. He was an old white man who put my metal into a basket and weighed it on a large scale. No matter how much I had collected, he would always say, "Ten pounds, three cents." But there wasn't no other buyer, so I took the three cents.

Since I wasn't gonna get my two dollars that way, I started running errands for the neighbors on Sundays. Mrs. Pooley was my best customer. One warm November morning I found her sitting in a rocker on her store's front porch. "Anything I can do for you today, ma'am?" I asked.

"Yes, Dit, there is." Beside her was a large sack, tied at one end with a bit of rope. She kicked at the sack with her foot. "I want you to take this sack and throw it in the river."

I looked at the sack. The bag moved and meowed loudly. "There're kittens in there."

Mrs. Pooley shrugged. "Maybe there are and maybe there ain't. In any case, I don't want them. You take them to the river and I'll give you a nickel."

"No, ma'am," I said politely. "I don't like the idea of drowning no kittens."

Mrs. Pooley pouted. "Now, Dit, are you gonna run errands for me or not?"

"Yes, ma'am."

"Then take this bag and throw it in the river."

"Aw, Mrs. Pooley, if it was snakes I wouldn't mind, but . . ."

Mrs. Pooley tsked loudly. "Buster'd probably do it."

"He's not half as responsible as me!"

"Chip, then."

"I need the money!" I protested. I rubbed the back of my head. My hair was growing in itchy and uneven, but I didn't dare ask Doc for another haircut.

"You drive a hard bargain, Dit," she said with a smile. "I'll make it a dime." She reached into her pocket and pressed a coin into my hand. "Now you take that bag, throw it in the river, and that's that!"

I swallowed and picked up the bag.

A few minutes later I stood on the bank of the Black Warrior, clutching the squirming sack. The meows got louder and louder till I couldn't hear nothing else. I peeked inside and saw two small kittens looking up at me. "Meow?" said one of them. I quickly closed the sack. My hands were sweating as I set the bag carefully down on the ground.

I shoved my hand into my pocket and pulled out the dime. It shined like an icicle in the sunlight. I hid it again in my pocket.

Slowly I picked up the bag and turned my back to the river. I closed my eyes and with a deep breath hurled the sack up over my head and into the water.

Took off running before I even heard the splash. Didn't stop till I reached Emma's. She and her family were just coming out the front door. "You going to church?" I asked.

"Yes," said Mrs. Walker.

"Mind if I come too?"

Mrs. Walker looked at me funny. "You already went to church, Dit. Saw you go with Raymond and the twins this morning."

I shrugged. "Feel like going again."

She nodded and I fell into step beside Emma. "Emma," I whispered. "I think I did something bad." I quickly told her about Mrs. Pooley and the kittens.

"Aw, Dit," Emma groaned. "Why'd you do it?"

"Mrs. Pooley said she wouldn't hire me no more if I didn't."

"You promised not to kill any more animals."

"Not for fun. But I gotta earn money for the Fourth hunt."

Emma shook her head. "Those poor little kittens."

We walked the rest of the way to church without talking.

26

✝

HOW LONG WILL HELL LAST?

THE NEGRA CHURCH WAS A SQUARE, wooden building. It was small but neat and tidy, with colorful flowers all along its sides. Inside were long rows of wooden pews. A simple cross hung above the altar, and there weren't no stained glass windows. Most of the worshipers were Negras, but there were a few white children here and there who had come with their maids. At my church, there were a lot more decorations and a lot fewer people. Puzzled over that for a minute as I squeezed into a pew with Emma and her family. Then I folded my hands in prayer and tried not to think about the kittens.

"Our sermon today," Reverend Cannon announced from the pulpit, "is entitled 'How Long Will Hell Last?'"

I gulped.

"Those who have been unjust and have inflicted suffering on those smaller and weaker than themselves will burn in hell," boomed the reverend.

I gripped the edge of the pew and watched as my hands turned white.

"Those who harm innocent creatures," the reverend continued, "will suffer in hell as surely as those who've broken all of the Ten Commandments."

I looked up.

"How long will this hell last?"

I didn't really want to know, but he went ahead and answered his own question.

"As long as it would take you to drop one grain of sand at a time into the ocean and use up all the sand in the world."

It seemed like he was staring right at me.

When a hat was passed around after Reverend Cannon was finally done, I didn't even hesitate before giving him my dime.

After church, I made Emma come with me to the river. "They're dead by now, Dit," Emma said.

I ignored her and continued to look out over the water.

"Let's go home. You won't do it again."

"That's what I said when I killed the buzzard," I pointed out. "I did do it again."

Emma shrugged. "You can't help it, Dit. You're just good at killing things."

"Don't say that!"

I scanned the water desperately. There was a log stuck between two rocks, bobbing in place in the weak current. On the log were two dark bumps. Could those be kittens?

I bundled Emma into a leaky canoe someone had abandoned on the riverbank. We quickly paddled out to the log. Sure enough, the two tiny kittens shivered and clung to the wood. They meowed loudly as we approached. God had worked a miracle in exchange for my dime.

Emma leaned out of the canoe and picked up one kitten,

placing it safely into the boat. As she leaned out to get the other, the canoe tipped and Emma fell into the water.

I leaned over to grab her but couldn't see her. "Emma?" Tiny bubbles broke the surface where she had fallen in. "Emma!" She can barely swim, I thought frantically.

I was about to jump in after her when Emma finally surfaced, five or six feet away. She doggy-paddled back to the boat just like Pearl had shown her. I pulled her back into the canoe.

She shivered uncontrollably. "You all right, Emma?"

"Cold," she mumbled. "The water's cold."

I pulled off my jacket and handed it to her.

"Dit?"

"What?"

Emma pointed. The log with the other kitten had broken free of the rock and was floating quickly away. Didn't even give it a second thought before I dove into the water.

Only took me four strong strokes to catch up with the log. Emma paddled the canoe over to me. I placed the kitten inside the canoe and then crawled back in over the edge. We stared at each other, dripping water.

"My mama's going to kill me," she moaned as she shivered in my jacket. "My good dress!"

"Least we'll both be in trouble for ruining our Sunday clothes," I said.

Emma smiled.

We took the kittens to our barn. Soon as I put them down in a pile of soft hay, they started to mew loudly.

"I think they're hungry," said Emma.

There was no way I was gonna sneak into the kitchen and

get some milk without my mama noticing. Luckily, Betsy, our oldest cow, had a sore foot and we hadn't driven her out to pasture that morning. So I went to her stall, sat down on the milking stool and squirted some milk into an old saucer. Soon as I put the saucer down, the kittens jumped on it, lapping away with their small pink tongues.

When I turned around, Emma was staring at me, amazed. "Can I try?" she asked.

"Ain't you ever milked no cow before?"

"No," said Emma. "The milkman brings the milk in Boston."

I figured we really couldn't do much else till our clothes dried, so I grabbed a bucket and sat Emma down on the stool.

"This here's the udder," I said. "There are four teats. You put your hand on one like so." I showed her how to pinch the teat with her fingers. "Then you pull down and squeeze and strip that milk right out."

Emma tried. Nothing happened. She pulled harder. Not a drop. Finally, Betsy mooed in protest and flicked Emma with her tail.

"Let me show you again," I said.

"I can do it," protested Emma. "Just stop mumbling. You're distracting me."

"I ain't talking," I said.

"Well, someone is," Emma said, and we both stopped to listen.

Sure enough, somebody was saying something, though we couldn't quite make out the words. It sounded like it was coming from the other end of the barn.

Me and Emma left Betsy in peace and crept down to the

empty stall nearest the door. The kittens followed us too, hoping for more milk.

The noises in the stall got louder as we approached. It sounded like two people, whispering and laughing. I threw open the stall door.

There, sitting on a bale of hay, was my oldest sister, Della. And she was kissing Mr. Fulton's oldest boy.

"Della!" I exclaimed.

Mr. Fulton's boy was so surprised he fell backwards off the bale of hay, right into a pile of cow dung.

I started to laugh. Even Emma had to fight back a giggle.

"What are you doing here?" Della asked. Her hair had fallen down off her head and there was hay in her braids. Her work apron was bunched up on the floor.

"What are you doing?" I asked. Della turned bright red, and that made me laugh even harder.

Mr. Fulton's boy jumped up and ran out of the barn so fast, he didn't even notice he had a big glob of cow poop stuck to the back of his head.

Della picked up her work apron and put it back on. She started to pick the hay out of her hair.

I grinned. "Wait till Mama finds out."

"You can't tell, Dit," Della pleaded. "Please, you can't."

"We won't tell anyone," said Emma.

"Speak for yourself," I said. "This is too darn funny to keep quiet!"

"We won't tell," continued Emma, "but you have to get us some clean clothes and wash and press the ones we have on."

Emma always was a step or two ahead of me.

For the first time, Della noticed that we were wet from head to toe.

"Sure," Della answered. "Give me half an hour. Only one question."

"What?" asked Emma.

"What were you two up to?"

The kittens peeked out from behind Emma's leg and gave a little meow.

27

A NEW JOB

TWO WEEKS BEFORE THANKSGIVING, DR. Griffith got a new Model T Ford sedan. It was a beautiful black car with shiny leather seats and a permanent top so you wouldn't ever get caught in the rain. I stopped to admire it on the way home from school. It didn't look nothing like my pa's old Ford.

Dr. Griffith came out of his house while I was standing there. "Hi, Dr. Griffith," I said. "Need any help starting your car?"

He shook his head. "You gotta be careful starting a car, Dit. You don't do it right, the crank can reverse and break your arm."

I knew this. Ulman had showed me at home. "I've been practicing."

"On my car? You been cranking it to hear the engine run and then cutting it off?"

"No."

"Your father's?" he asked.

"Maybe."

Dr. Griffith sighed. "Go ahead. Let's see what you can do."

He climbed into the front seat. I bent over and cranked the engine. Did it pretty well if I do say so myself. The engine soon began to purr. I grinned.

The doctor looked me over. "Get in, Dit," he said finally.

"Why?"

"I drive into Selma once a month to pick up supplies. Takes about four hours each way. I could use someone to help with the driving. You interested in the job?"

I couldn't wipe the smile off my face.

Only took a couple of days for Dr. Griffith to teach me to drive. I catch on fast to things like that. Pretty soon I could start the car, drive it a ways and make it come to a jerky stop. But that wasn't enough for Dr. Griffith. He lectured me on safety too, and when a man was killed three miles north of Moundville on the Tuscaloosa road, he made me go look at the body.

"It was raining and he was going too fast for the muddy road," Dr. Griffith told me. "I want you to see what happens when a car turns over."

The body was covered with a sheet. Dr. Griffith pulled the sheet back and I saw the man's face. He lay perfectly still with his eyes wide open.

It wasn't the first time I had seen the face of a dead man. Once, before I even had my nickname, Pa had taken me to a funeral and lifted me up so I could see inside the casket. The teenage boy inside was all dressed up in a clean suit. I thought he looked real nice. "That's Eli," said Pa. "He's dead." I later learned Eli Howell had been cleaning his gun when it accidentally went off. Least that's what some people said. Others whispered he had killed himself but his mama convinced the doctor to say it was an accident so he could still be buried in the churchyard. So even though it wasn't the first time I had seen a dead man, it was the first time I understood what I was seeing. And it gave me the creeps.

Dr. Griffith wasn't satisfied till I could change the oil, mend a flat and change gears as smooth as ice skating. But finally, he leaned back in his seat and smiled. "I think you're ready. You're a smart boy, Dit."

"Thank you, sir."

"Why hasn't your father taught you how to drive?"

I shrugged. "We only got one car. Pa, Ulman, Elman and Raymond can all drive. We don't need no more drivers."

Dr. Griffith nodded.

But as I was walking home that afternoon, I didn't feel as excited as I expected. Dr. Griffith was awfully nice, but he wasn't my pa.

28

I MAKE MRS. WALKER
REAL, REAL MAD

I HATE TO ADMIT IT, BUT MRS. SEAY WAS A good teacher. I ain't never worked so dang hard. While the old schoolteacher, Mr. Summons, just droned on and on, reading from notes that had yellowed with age, Mrs. Seay found ways to make me forget I was learning.

On the Tuesday before Thanksgiving, Mrs. Seay invited Uncle Wiggens to come tell us about his experiences during the War Between the States. He stood at the front of the classroom, balancing on his one good leg and gesturing wildly as he spoke. "And then Sherman marched his army through Georgia and burned everything in his way. Churches, schools, even hospitals, just burned them up like they was kindling."

Everyone leaned forward, eyes wide.

"Then the Union forces burned the University of Alabama." Uncle Wiggens opened and closed his fists, wriggling his fingers. I think they were supposed to be the flames, licking at the buildings. "The Yankees didn't want you to have no education. If it hadn't been for General Lee, that's Robert E. Lee, mind you, none of you would be here today!"

All the kids gasped. Course we had all heard Uncle

Wiggens's stories a million times before, but Mrs. Seay was new in town and didn't know that. We were smart enough to figure we'd best put on a good show for her or she'd send Uncle Wiggens home and make us go back to arithmetic.

"And when they won the war, the Yankees freed all the Negras. Talk about stamping on Southern honor! Why, those gosh darn son of a—"

"Now, Uncle Wiggens," said Mrs. Seay, standing up quickly. "This is a school."

Pearl and a couple of the other girls giggled nervously.

"But ma'am, it could happen again. Those Yankees could—"

"No one is going to burn down our school," Mrs. Seay said firmly. "Especially since we have a good lawman like Big Foot protecting our town."

"I'm sorry, ma'am," Uncle Wiggens said sheepishly, rubbing at the place where his wooden leg attached to his stump. "It just makes me so angry, I sometimes get carried away."

Mrs. Seay brought over a chair and helped him sit down. "It is upsetting to think about the time we lost the best of a whole generation."

I was still imagining dying soldiers that evening after supper when I went over to Emma's. We usually did our homework together while Mrs. Walker washed the dishes. Emma made me repeat just about every little thing that happened at school so she could learn it too. I said I didn't ask her to tell me everything she learned at her school, but Emma just rolled her eyes and told me to get on with it.

So I started telling Emma about General Sherman and him burning schools. Even wiggled my hands like Uncle Wiggens. But when I got to the part about us losing the best of a whole generation, Mrs. Walker jumped in. "What did you say, Dit?"

"I was just telling Emma what Mrs. Seay said," I explained. "About how sad it was that the South lost the war."

"Sad for whom?" Suds dripped off Mrs. Walker's hands and onto the floor, but she didn't seem to notice.

"Why, for everyone."

"Maybe to men like Uncle Wiggens it was a sad day," Mrs. Walker hollered, "but not for us Negroes! Dit, do you have any idea where we'd be if the South hadn't lost the war?"

My hands were sweating. I'd never even heard Mrs. Walker raise her voice before. "Back in Boston?"

"Picking cotton on a plantation in South Carolina!" She threw down her dishrag and began to pace the room.

"Your great-grandmother used to get up before sunrise and work in the fields all day without a rest," Mrs. Walker said to Emma. "If she didn't work fast enough, she was whipped until the blood ran down her back. That could have been your fate."

"I know, Mama," Emma said quietly.

I tried to picture it, but it was hard. I could see Buster in the fields or even myself, but Emma?

"After that war was over, my grandmother and her children and their children could hold their heads up high and be treated like people instead of animals!"

I shook my head. "But Mrs. Seay said—"

"I don't care what she said! The day the Confederate army surrendered was a good day." She picked up the wet rag from the floor. "You'd better go home now, Dit."

Emma walked me to the door. "What'd I say?" I whispered. I liked Mrs. Walker and felt bad that I upset her. Also, she made the best biscuits in town.

Emma shrugged. "You just repeated what Mrs. Seay said."

"Then why's she so angry?"

Emma bit her lower lip. "Maybe Mrs. Seay's wrong."

I shook my head. "She's a good teacher, Emma. You said so yourself. Ain't that why you make me repeat everything she says?"

"Even the smartest people make mistakes," Emma insisted.

I thought maybe I just didn't explain it right, so we decided to meet up the next day after school and talk to Mrs. Seay. Surely the teacher could explain things so that Emma would understand.

But that night in bed, I did some more thinking. Big Foot had been wrong to steal that hair tonic from Doc Haley. And Mrs. Pooley shouldn't have told me to drown those kittens. It was just possible, I decided, that Mrs. Seay was wrong about the war.

29

A DAY IN JAIL

THE WILSON SCHOOL WAS TWO MILES away, so when Mrs. Seay let us out the next day, I sat down under a tree to wait for Emma. I was planning on taking a little nap when Chip walked up to me. "Hey, Dit," he said.

"Hi," I said. Chip had hardly spoken to me since he'd switched desks.

"Haven't seen you around much," said Chip.

"No."

"Baseball's not as fun without our best pitcher." Chip grinned, showing off his straight, white teeth.

I looked at him suspiciously. "You trying to be nice?"

"And what if I am?" said Chip. "We been friends a long time."

That was true enough.

"Come on," said Chip. "I want to show you something."

"What?"

"It's a surprise."

"Nah." I had to wait for Emma.

"Why not?" asked Chip.

"I'm meeting someone."

"That Negra girl?" Chip asked.

"No." But I think he knew I was lying.

"Aw, come on, Dit," said Chip. "It'll just take a minute."

He was being nice. Besides, I would probably be back before Emma came.

"All right," I said finally, and stood up to follow him.

Chip led me over to city hall. It was an old wooden building, not much used, but Chip's pa had an office there. The back door was open and we crept into the basement.

"What you want to show me?" I asked. "There's only spiders and rats here."

"You'll see," Chip said.

I took a few steps forward, almost bumping into Chip when he stopped in front of an old jail cell. "Here we are," he announced.

The old jail hadn't been used in years. Weren't too many crimes committed in Moundville. It's kind of hard to break the law when everybody knows your business. "Why'd you bring me here?"

Buster stepped out of the darkness. "We wanted to play a little baseball," he said. He glanced at Chip and together they shoved me into the cell. Before I could scramble to my feet, Buster slammed the door.

The floor was dusty and I sneezed. "Why didn't you just ask," I said, wiping my dirty hands on my pants. "I'd be happy to give you another bloody nose."

Buster snickered. The sound bounced off the dark walls till it sounded like a thousand tiny mice squealing at me.

I stood up and tried the door. It was locked. "You're gonna get in big trouble," I said, trying to keep my voice calm. "Go get Big Foot. He'll have the key."

"We don't need Big Foot," Buster said.

"Then how you gonna get me out?"

Chip pulled out a key on a string around his neck. "My dad's the mayor."

Of course. Chip would have it all planned out. "Fine," I said. "You had your joke. Now let me out."

"Not till you say it," Buster growled.

"Say what?" I taunted. "How much I want to beat you up again?"

"You gotta admit you love that nigger girl," said Chip.

"I do not!"

"Then we won't let you out," said Buster. Chip tucked the key back under his shirt.

It was probably only an hour or so, but it seemed like forever. Buster and Chip sat on the stairs, watching me. I crossed my arms and stared back at them. I wasn't gonna speak first.

"Come on, Dit," Chip said finally. "It's getting cold down here."

"I ain't gonna say it." I wasn't cold. I was steaming. My "best friend" had locked me in a jail cell.

"Then we'll let the rats eat your bones," said Buster, sounding a little tired.

We sat in silence a while longer. There were rats, and I watched a fat one make a nest in the corner of the cell. "I got to get home," I said finally. "It's past time for chores."

"You hang out with her sometimes, right?" asked Chip. Guess he was tiring of the game.

"Yes."

"Say she's your very best friend and we'll let you out."

I considered this. I didn't like admitting it, but I didn't like being locked in a cell even more. "All right. Emma's my very best friend."

Buster snickered again. But this time it sounded hollow.

Chip took the key from around his neck and shrugged. "Anyway, I got to get the key back before my dad notices."

Chip unlocked the door. I stepped out of the cell and swung at him. Didn't even realize how angry I was at him till my fist was in the air. I understood why Buster was upset—I'd beat him up in front of everyone. But Chip was my friend. We'd pulled a hundred tricks like this together. And the truth was, till now, I'd never given a thought to what it was like to be the one on the other side.

My fist hit Chip square in the jaw. He fell to the ground. Buster bent down to help him. I ran up the stairs and didn't look back.

That night, I didn't go over to Emma's. Me and Pearl sat at the dining room table doing our homework. About a quarter to eight, there was a knock at our door. I didn't move. There was another knock. Finally, Pearl slid off her chair and went to answer it.

She returned a moment later with Emma. "Where were you today?" Emma asked.

I wanted to tell her about Chip and Buster, felt the words building up like a pressure in my chest. But I didn't know what to say. Me and Chip had been friends for just about forever and suddenly everything had changed. "I forgot," I lied. "I'm sorry."

"Oh, it's all right," she said. "I just introduced myself to Mrs. Seay." She put a huge book down on the table.

"What's that?" I asked.

Emma smiled. "I told her I thought she was wrong about the war. She pulled out this old book and told me if I read the whole thing and wrote an essay on it, she'd discuss the issue with me further."

Pearl laughed. "She thought you wouldn't do it!"

"No." Emma grinned, fire sparkling in her brown eyes. "She thought I couldn't read!"

Course Emma started on the book that very night. First, she read the entire table of contents. Out loud. Me and Pearl 'bout fell asleep, but Emma said it was important to know where the book was going. I said that book was too heavy to go anywhere. Emma rolled her eyes and turned the page to chapter one.

30

THANKSGIVING

THE NEXT DAY WAS THANKSGIVING, AND Mama woke us all before dawn. There was a lot to do if we were gonna eat at noon. Why we had to eat at noon was beyond me, but you didn't argue with Mama, especially on a holiday.

While Mama and the girls were busy cooking the turkey, shelling peas and baking pies, Pa and us boys scrubbed the floors and washed the windows, in addition to all the normal chores like chopping wood and milking the cows. Even little Robert and Lois helped Mama get out the good tablecloth and set the table. We usually ate in shifts, but on holidays Pa moved the card table from the parlor into the dining room and we all squeezed in together.

Right in the middle of the turkey, Pa asked if anyone had anything they were thankful for. Della gushed on and on 'bout Mr. Fulton's boy and how he was gonna ask for her hand any day now. Ollie liked the new dress she'd got for her birthday, Ulman was grateful for Mama's mashed potatoes, Elman was thrilled he hadn't failed his math test and Raymond was thankful for the pumpkin pie he could smell in the kitchen.

Finally, it was my turn. I cleared my throat, just like Mrs. Seay did when she was trying to make sure everyone was listening. "I'm thankful for my new job."

"You got a job?" said Pa. He sounded surprised, and I thought a little proud too. "Doing what?"

"Driving Dr. Griffith into Selma. He's got to go once a month to pick up supplies."

"Driving?" said Elman. "Dit don't know how to drive."

"I do now," I said. "Dr. Griffith taught me."

"Why'd he do that?" said Raymond. "Could have just asked one of us."

I'd wondered the same thing myself. "Guess he likes me better."

Raymond threw a pat of butter at me.

"Boys!" Mama said sharply. "This is my good tablecloth!"

Pa shook his head. "So my boy knows how to drive. Well, I'll be—"

But just when he was about to say something nice (or at least I think he was), Robert decided to imitate Raymond and throw a pat of butter. Only he knocked over his glass of milk instead. It spilled all over the tablecloth. Mama started wailing, so Ollie jumped up to get a towel, but she ran into Della, who'd had the same idea, and they knocked over a chair. Then Pearl reached for a drumstick and tipped over the green beans, and Earl started whining 'cause he wanted a drumstick and there weren't no more left, and the subject of me driving didn't come up again.

That evening me and Emma sat down on our front porch. She had eaten dinner with her family over at the church. I was complaining about my family and how loud they were and how I never got to say nothing and how irritating and—

134

"I don't know, Dit," Emma interrupted. "It doesn't sound so bad to me."

"That's 'cause you don't have any brothers or sisters."

"Yeah." She bit her lip.

"What?"

"I think my mama always wanted more children."

"Why you think that?"

"Once, when I was real little, she told me I was gonna have a brother or sister. Then a couple weeks later, Daddy had to get the doctor in the middle of the night. They never said anything more about it after that. They thought I forgot 'cause I was so small, but I didn't."

"Oh," I said.

Emma shrugged. "Reverend Cannon says we ought to be thankful for what we do have instead of cursing what we don't." She sighed. "It's not always so easy."

"Least we both got families," I said. "Think about poor Jim Dang-It, out in that cabin all alone."

We looked at each other.

"Do you think your mama has an extra pie?" asked Emma.

"Shoot, Emma," I said. "My mama has so many, I could steal one and she wouldn't even notice."

"We brought home some extra chicken from the church."

"Think Jim would mind some visitors?" I asked.

"There's one way to find out."

So that's how me and Emma found ourselves knocking on the door of Jim Dang-It's cabin late that night.

"What you dang kids want?" Jim growled as he pulled the door open.

"We brought you dinner," said Emma. "Happy Thanksgiving."

Jim broke into a grin, bigger than two arms held wide. "In that case, come on in."

"It ain't much," I said as we sat down at his tiny table in front of the fire.

"Just some chicken and an apple pie," Emma added.

Jim Dang-It was thoughtful for a moment. "An Indian, a Negra and a white boy sitting down to share some chicken and an apple pie." He nodded. "Sounds like a pretty good Thanksgiving to me."

And it was.

31

SELMA

ME AND DR. GRIFFITH SET OFF EARLY THE
next Saturday on our first trip to Selma. We were lucky—it
was sunny and hadn't rained for a while, so the roads were
good. In towns, people spread gravel on the roads to keep
down the mud, but in between the towns, there was only hard-
packed dirt.

Dr. Griffith let me drive the first half of the trip. I liked
driving, mainly 'cause it took all my concentration and I
couldn't worry 'bout nothing else. When we switched drivers,
Dr. Griffith said I had done a great job. "I might even let you
drive alone one of these days." I smiled so big, I thought the
skin on my cheeks was gonna split.

We got to Selma just before noon. Selma is an old wealthy
town that saw lots of action during the War Between the
States. About eighteen thousand people live there. I bet Emma
could figure out how many times bigger than Moundville that
is, but if you ask me, all that matters is that it's real big. I had
only been to Selma once before, and I was so little, I couldn't
remember much.

Me and Dr. Griffith ate lunch at the drugstore, where he

bought me a hamburger and a root beer float. When we were done eating, Dr. Griffith went to pick up his orders and I wandered around Main Street. Next to the drugstore was a fancy hotel. On the other side of the hotel was a general goods store, three times the size of Mrs. Pooley's. After that was an ice cream parlor. They had a room in the basement where they made the ice cream, and the man behind the counter told me I could go watch. It was cold as a winter morning in that room, all year long.

Across the street from the ice cream parlor was Pearson's Pool Hall. There was a big sign in the window that read, No One Under 21 Admitted. Maybe Chip wasn't lying about the pool hall after all. I was just getting ready to sneak inside myself when Dr. Griffith walked up and said it was time to go.

We were back in Moundville before suppertime. He gave me four dimes for the day's work, even though I would have gladly driven the car for free. I was gonna enter the Fourth hunt next year, and I was gonna win.

But the dimes reminded me of the one Mrs. Pooley had given me for getting rid of the kittens. The Fourth hunt wasn't the same thing at all. I knew that. Drowning kittens was just wasteful, and the Fourth hunt, well, it was a tradition. It was how we knew who was the best hunter in town, and hunting was important 'cause that's how people got their meat. Besides, how else was I gonna get Pa to stop calling me "Della, Ollie, Ulman, Elman, Raymond, uh, I mean Dit"?

Monday was gonna be my first day back at school since Chip and Buster had locked me in jail. I was so nervous, I woke up before dawn. My hands were sweating as I did my chores, and I dropped a bucket of coal all over the clean kitchen floor.

"Dit!" Ollie cried. It was her job to clean the floor.

"Sorry," I said. I wiped my hands on my pants as she passed me a broom to sweep up.

I hardly touched my eggs at breakfast, which meant more for my brothers, so Raymond and Earl could tell something was wrong too. On the way to school, I finally broke down and told them what had happened.

Raymond pounded his fist into the palm of his hand. "I'll teach Chip a lesson."

"No," I said. "I just want to forget about the whole thing."

"I'll protect you, Dit," said Earl. "Just let those two bullies try anything again."

My little brother was hardly strong enough to wrestle a squirrel, but I appreciated the thought.

Course after all that worrying and fretting, nothing happened. Chip and Buster just left me alone. At recess I played marbles with Earl and Raymond and gave Pearl and Mary piggyback rides. It actually turned out to be a real nice day.

That evening, I was over at Emma's, eating Mrs. Walker's biscuits again. I guess she had forgiven me. I was the only one who could get Emma to stop reading that dang history book for more than a few minutes at a time.

"I ain't working for Mrs. Pooley no more," I said casually, pretending to focus on my math homework.

"You're not?" Emma sounded interested, but she didn't take her eyes from the book.

"No. I got a job driving into Selma for Dr. Griffith."

"Oh." She was still reading.

"I want to be good at something 'sides killing things."

Emma put down her book. "You are good at other things," she said.

"Like what?"

"Skipping stones. Baseball." A curl escaped from her braid and hung right over her eyes.

I shook my head. "Something important."

Emma bit her lip. "You're good at being my friend."

"Is that important?" I asked.

"Yes," she said quietly. "It sure is."

I saw her looking at me. Without thinking, I brushed the curl out of her eyes.

She looked away.

Had I upset her? I didn't know what to say. So I simply picked up my pencil and did some more long division.

32

CHRISTMAS

THE WEEK BEFORE CHRISTMAS, ULMAN, Elman, Raymond, me, Earl and Pa went out into the forest to cut down a pine tree. Got the biggest one we could find. It took all five of us boys to carry it home. While we were gone, Mama and the girls popped corn over the coals in the kitchen. They strung the popped corn into large ropes, with bright red cranberries spaced in between the kernels. Mama had a set of eight porcelain bells that she had gotten as a wedding present. Only she was allowed to hang them on the tree. When no one was looking, I'd flick a bell with my finger to hear the tiny ring.

Reverend Cannon at the Negra church had found out Emma could play piano, so she spent the week before Christmas practicing on the church organ for the Christmas Eve service. I snuck inside and listened to her. She was much better than old Mrs. Weeks, who played at our church.

One day Emma saw me sitting in the back row of the pews. "Dit," she exclaimed. "I got you a Christmas present."

"What?" I asked.

"It's a surprise!"

I started to worry. If she had a present for me, I'd have to get a present for her. Thought long and hard about what to get Emma. In my family, we just got stuff in our stockings. I didn't have enough money to buy her something real special, like a new book. If I bought her something small and girly, like a handkerchief or some perfume, someone was sure to see me in Mrs. Pooley's store. Word would get back to Chip or Buster, and that would set me up for a lot more grief. So I decided to make her a twine baseball. After all, I was teaching her how to play.

I went to Mrs. Pooley's store and bought the small rubber ball we used as the base for five cents. A roll of twine was only ten cents more, so that wasn't much gone from my Fourth hunt money. Best of all, I could work on the present in front of anyone—even Emma—and no one would think a thing about it.

I wound the twine carefully, trying to make it even on all sides. Raymond was really better at winding balls than me, but I wanted to do this one myself. When I was finished, I wrapped it in a piece of old newspaper and hid it under my bed.

On Christmas Eve we all took a bath, just like it was Saturday evening. Right after supper, we all went to church. The preacher kept talking about the Star of Bethlehem and how amazed the shepherds had been when they had seen it. Our preacher wasn't as enthusiastic as Reverend Cannon at Emma's church, but I tried to pay attention. I didn't want to accidentally end up going to hell. But the Christmas candles were so pretty and the pine wreaths smelled so nice, all I could think of was, I sure hope I get some candy in my stocking. When Mrs. Weeks started playing, it didn't sound half as good as Emma, and I started wondering if she would like her present. It was Christmas after all. Surely God would understand if my mind wandered just a little.

The next morning our stockings were filled with oranges and peppermint sticks. Oranges in winter were something special, and I savored each juicy section. For breakfast there was sausage, ribbon cane syrup, hot light biscuits and all the fresh butter and sweet milk you could eat. Pa made a big wood fire in the parlor. Usually we used coal to heat our rooms, so the flames and popping of the wood made things seem special. We roasted pecans over the fire and sucked on our peppermint candy.

In the afternoon, I snuck out to meet Emma at our cave. I got there first and sat clutching the lumpy, newspaper-wrapped package in my lap. There was a chill in the air. I'd grabbed one of Raymond's old sweaters, but there were patches on the elbows and the cold leaked in, causing me to shiver.

"Merry Christmas!" exclaimed Emma as she ducked into the cave.

"Hi," I said. She had on a new red coat. The hood was trimmed with white fur.

"Open it! Open it!" she squealed, thrusting a package wrapped in green tissue paper into my hands. "I can't wait any longer!"

I was pretty curious myself, so I tore off the green paper fast as can be. It was a brand-new, spanking-clean baseball. I forgot about being cold.

"Emma . . ." I started, but nothing else came out.

"Turn it over," she said, grinning.

I turned the ball over. On the other side, in clear black ink, was a signature. Walter Johnson. I stared.

"Do you like it?" Emma asked. "Last month I asked my daddy who was the greatest baseball pitcher around and he said Walter Johnson. So I wrote Mr. Johnson a letter and told him my best friend was a big, big baseball fan and could he please, please, please send him a signed baseball for Christmas. The package came last week, and I just about burst waiting to give it to you. Do you like it?"

"Emma . . ." I said again, but I couldn't go on.

"You like it!" she said, breaking into a huge smile.

Like it? This was the nicest thing anyone had ever done for me, and all I had for her was an old twine baseball. I was embarrassed, but there was nothing else to do 'cept hand over my poorly wrapped package.

Emma unfolded the newspaper carefully. "Oh, Dit," she sighed when she saw the ball. "Did you make this for me?"

I nodded.

She picked up the baseball. "My very own baseball." She pressed it to her heart. "This is about the sweetest thing anyone's ever done for me."

"It's just an old baseball," I said. But she insisted on gushing over it, like it was made of pure gold. It wasn't till we were outside throwing the twine baseball back and forth that I finally believed Emma liked her present too.

That evening, the whole town lined up along Main Street. Me and Emma showed off our new baseballs to just about everyone. Even Chip and Buster didn't tease us, just said, "Merry Christmas," and kept on walking. When it got dark, Pa and Dr. Griffith shot off fireworks. The beautiful red and yellow and green sparkles in the sky must have looked just like the Star of Bethlehem looked to the shepherds in the field.

33

THE FAMOUS
DING LING CIRCUS

WHEN I WALKED INTO SCHOOL AFTER THE
Christmas holidays, the words *The Famous Ding Ling Circus*
were written on the board. I was real glad that we were doing
something different 'cause maybe that would help me smooth
over my problems with Chip and Buster. Don't get me wrong,
I was still mad—especially at Chip. I knew we'd never be
friends like we were before, but Moundville was too small to
ignore them forever.

Mrs. Seay stood in front of the class, a broad smile on her
face. "This year, we are going to put on a play," she announced.
"*The Famous Ding Ling Circus* is about a Chinaman who
comes to the United States to put on a circus and becomes
rich and famous. Everyone will have a part, and it's going to be
lots of fun."

I was excited. Pa had taken Della to the circus when she
was little. For years when she put us younger kids to bed, she
told us stories of the acrobats and clowns and lions and tigers
and elephants. I had always wanted to go to the circus myself,
but it didn't often come to Alabama. Being in a play about a
circus was almost as good.

Mrs. Seay wrote the names of all the roles on the board and started to assign parts. Pearl got to be the tightrope ballerina, and Raymond volunteered to be a cowboy. I had my eye on the lion tamer and was waiting for Mrs. Seay to get to that part.

"Now we also need a ringmaster," said Mrs. Seay. "This is the starring role."

Of course, no one raised their hand. Who wanted to learn all those lines?

"Come on," Mrs. Seay coaxed. "This is the great Ding Ling, come all the way from China to seek his fortune."

I slumped down further in my seat.

"Well, someone has to do it." Mrs. Seay tapped her pearls with her ruler. "Chip, how about you?"

"No way!" said Chip. "I don't want to be no Chinaman with slitty eyes!"

The class laughed.

"Then you, Dit." She pointed the ruler at me.

"But I want to be the lion tamer!" I protested.

"Chip can do that part. You'll be the ringmaster." And it was settled just like that. Chip glanced over at me and grinned. I looked away.

After school, I trudged up to Mrs. Seay's desk.

"Mrs. Seay, I really don't want to be the ringmaster."

"Dit, I'm sure you can do it. You're one of my best students." She didn't even look up from her papers.

"No, I ain't," I said. "You only think so 'cause Emma helps me with my homework."

Mrs. Seay looked up. "That little Negra girl?"

I nodded. "There's no way I'm gonna be able to learn all those lines."

146

"Well, I'm sorry, Dit, but you're going to have to try." She gave me a smile and went back to her papers.

Over the next few weeks, I spent hours at the Walker kitchen table, studying my script while Emma read the large history book. Most of our evenings went something like this:

"Welcome, ladies and gentlemen, to the most fabulous . . ."

"Fantastical," Emma corrected, not even looking up from her book.

". . . most fantastical circus of the year."

"Of the century." Emma turned a page of her book.

I looked at her and frowned. "How come you know my lines?"

"I've heard you repeat them often enough," she said.

"Go back to your own work."

Emma smiled and continued reading.

Finally, I admitted that going over my lines once a day was not enough. So in the afternoons, me and Emma started studying in our cave. It was late January, but not too cold. Emma wore her pretty red coat, and I just threw an old blanket around me. She would hold the script, and I was supposed to say my lines. It usually went more like this:

"Now turn your attention to the death-dying—"

"No," Emma interrupted. "Now turn your attention to the death-defying . . ."

"Now turn your attention to the death-defying tightrope walkers, who . . ." I stopped.

"Who what?"

"I don't remember."

". . . who will dazzle your eyes with their feats of balance!"

I grabbed the script from Emma and threw it down. "I only wanted to be the lion tamer." I took a soda from our stash. "Read me some of your essay."

Emma had finished reading the fat history book and was now working on her essay for Mrs. Seay. It was good. Real good. Course she made it sound all smooth and flowery, but the point was this: during the war, both sides did bad things. Sherman was wrong to burn the homes and businesses of innocent people. But the war also brought freedom to millions of Negras. It forced us to come together as one country. And even though I was from the South, Emma's essay made me decide that I was glad the Union had won the war.

I clapped when she finished reading the paper. Emma played with a corner of her paper. "Stop teasing me, Dit."

"I'm not teasing," I said. "It's real good."

Emma smiled. "Tomorrow, I'm going to give it to Mrs. Seay." Her smile slowly faded. "If that's okay with you."

"Of course." I wanted to see Mrs. Seay's face when she realized how smart Emma was.

"But Chip and Buster . . ."

"What about them?"

"I don't want you to end up in jail again."

"How'd you hear about that?" I'd never mentioned it.

"People talk."

I waved my hand in the air. "I don't care about them," I lied.

Emma smiled again. "Thanks, Dit."

I got up to go home.

"Dit," Emma called out.

I stopped in the mouth of our cave.

"You're my very best friend too."

And just like that, my lie was true. I really didn't care about Chip or Buster. Who needed them when I had a friend like Emma.

34

THE LION TAMER

THE NEXT DAY MRS. SEAY ASKED EVERYONE
to stay after school to rehearse the play. It was almost the end
of January, and no one was even close to knowing their lines.
"Let's take it from page five," she said. Her dress wasn't quite
as crisp as it had been that morning, and even her hat was a
little out of shape.

I flipped through my copy of the script. "Where?"

"From the lion tamer's entrance." Mrs. Seay tugged at her
necklace. I think she was beginning to regret ever having come
up with the idea of doing a play in the first place.

"We ain't got no lion tamer," said Pearl.

"What?" asked Mrs. Seay.

"Chip's not here," Raymond explained.

"Wasn't he here this morning?" asked Mrs. Seay.

"He went home at lunchtime," I said. "Said his stomach
hurt."

Mrs. Seay sent Raymond to Chip's house to find out what
was going on. Turned out Chip was in bed with appendicitis.
Dr. Griffith told his mama she had better send him down to
the hospital in Selma. "They're gonna cut him open and rip out

his appendix," Raymond reported. "He won't be back to school for a long time."

Don't get me wrong, I didn't want him to die or nothing. But I was a little bit glad.

Mrs. Seay took off her hat and put it down on her desk. "So now we need a lion tamer."

"I can be the lion tamer," I said. "Watch as I bravely put my head into the ferocious beast's mouth. I pet his mane and he purrs like a kitten." That was the one part I could always remember.

"I'm not being the lion if he's the lion tamer," said Buster.

"Dit's the ringmaster," said Mrs. Seay. She tugged at her necklace again. Must have been a little too hard, because there was a tiny pop and pearls flew everywhere. Mrs. Seay gasped, and her mouth hung open in a small *O*. She looked like she was gonna cry as she knelt down and began to gather up the beads.

Just then, the school door opened and Emma entered. Everyone turned to look at her. She blinked and forced on a brave smile.

"What do you want?" Mrs. Seay snapped from the floor.

"I just wanted to return your book and give you my essay." Emma pulled the thick book out of her bag and placed it on a desk. Then she held out her essay, her neat black handwriting shiny on the white paper.

Mrs. Seay looked lost. She struggled to her feet, the loose pearls clutched in one hand.

"On the War Between the States," Emma prompted. "Don't you remember?"

"You read this entire book?" asked Mrs. Seay, pointing to the desk.

"Of course!" exclaimed Emma. "You told me not to come back until I did." Emma glanced at me. I didn't know what to say.

"We're rehearsing our play now," said Mrs. Seay.

Buster pointed at Emma and whispered something to Sally. She turned to Jill. They were already gossiping about her. But I didn't care what they thought, right? Emma was my friend and I was gonna be brave and defend her. If only I could think of something to say.

Mrs. Seay was still talking. ". . . and this is really not a good time to . . ."

Emma was watching me like she was drowning and I had promised to throw her a rope, only I was standing on the riverbank watching her sink into the water.

". . . come here and think I could stop my lessons with my real students to—"

"She can be my prompter," I interrupted.

"We don't have any more scripts," said Mrs. Seay.

"Oh, I don't need a script," said Emma.

"Little girl," Mrs. Seay said sharply, "it's not polite to brag."

"Her name's Emma," I said, "and she's not bragging." Felt like I was jumping off a cliff as I said that, right in front of everyone. Sure there was gonna be a big splash as Sally and Jill started talking about me. But there wasn't no splash. They just stopped whispering and looked at Emma.

Mrs. Seay folded her arms. "Then what does the ringmaster say when the clown enters?"

Emma cleared her throat. "Now put your hands together and welcome Hairy Larry to the stage. His nose might be red and his hair blue, but his funny bone is screwed on just right."

Mrs. Seay looked down at the script. "How about the elephant trainer? What's his line?"

"When I hit them with my whip, the pachyderms like to dance and dip," Emma rattled off.

"A pack of worms?" asked Buster. Expected him to say something more, but guess he wasn't as brave without Chip.

Mrs. Seay uncrossed her arms. "What about when the acrobats make their entrance?"

"The first or second time?" asked Emma.

That's when Mrs. Seay finally started to smile.

35

I OVERHEAR
A CONVERSATION

WE RAN ALL THE WAY HOME TO TELL MAMA
and Mrs. Walker the good news. The play had been retitled
The Famous African Princess Circus, and Emma was gonna be
the ringmaster. I was gonna be the lion tamer, and Mrs. Seay
had told Buster he still had to be the lion.

But Mama and Mrs. Walker were not as pleased as we expected. In fact, Mrs. Walker took Emma's arm and marched
her inside, saying something about it being time for supper. But
Mr. Walker didn't get home till six, and it wasn't even four
thirty. I asked Mama if we were eating early too and she just
shook her head. At eight Emma came over and asked me to tell
Mrs. Seay her mama didn't want her in the play.

Mrs. Seay frowned when I delivered Emma's message, but she
didn't say nothing. Didn't even make us practice the play. I was
almost happy to get back to math and reading, long as it meant
I didn't have to struggle through the ringmaster's lines.

That evening I was at Emma's writing out my spelling words
when there was a knock at the door. Mrs. Walker put down
her sewing and went to answer it. It was Mrs. Seay. Mrs.

Walker led her into the parlor and shut the door. I glanced at Emma and without a word, we both slid off our chairs and put our ears to the door.

Now, I don't try to listen to other people's conversations. I know it ain't polite. But sometimes what they are saying is so dang interesting, it's not my fault if I accidentally on purpose listen in.

"Did you read the essay Emma wrote?" I heard Mrs. Seay say through the door.

"No," answered Mrs. Walker.

"You didn't help her with it at all?"

"I didn't know she was writing it."

"It was better than the work of students twice her age. Why, she almost had me convinced that losing the war was a good thing—and I'm a Southern girl, born and bred."

"Emma's not going to be in the play. I thought she asked Dit to tell you. I'm sorry you came all this way."

"Did you hear what I just said?" asked Mrs. Seay.

"Yes. Did you hear me?" Mrs. Walker's voice was cold. They sat in silence for a long moment.

"I can't believe I'm asking this," Mrs. Seay said slowly, "but please let your daughter be in our play."

"I can't."

"Why not?"

"You wouldn't understand."

"Don't you think it's hard for me to ask a Negra for help?" Mrs. Seay snapped.

We heard Mrs. Walker stand up and march toward the door. Me and Emma scrambled quickly back to the table.

"Mrs. Walker, I don't always say the right thing," Mrs. Seay called out. "But most of us in Alabama, we're not bad people."

Mrs. Walker must have had her hand on the doorknob, 'cause it started to turn. Me and Emma pretended to concentrate on our homework. "Tell that to the poor Negro who was lynched in Jefferson County last month," we heard Mrs. Walker call out.

"I said most of us. Not all."

There was a long pause. "So what are you proposing?" Mrs. Walker said finally.

"I've never worked with a Negra child before," Mrs. Seay said brightly, "but I can't see how she's so much different than the rest. The play is supposed to go on in less than a month. No one knows the lines except Emma."

"No."

"Fine. Then you tell her she can't play the role because she's a Negra."

Emma grinned and squeezed my hand. That was the one thing Mrs. Walker would never do. And sure enough, the next morning Mrs. Walker told Emma she had changed her mind.

36

THE BIRTHDAY SURPRISE

WE STARTED HAVING REHEARSALS EVERY day after school. I was excited Emma was gonna be in the play, but a little nervous too. The other kids knew Emma from the baseball field, of course, but there she was just the little Negra girl who couldn't hit the ball. How would they react when they realized she was so smart? Would they think she was stuck-up? Call her teacher's pet?

I got real worried that first day when Emma started talking about how easy it was to learn her lines. That's not too good a way to make people like you. Then she started chatting with Mrs. Seay about reading and books. I knew she was a bookworm, but she didn't have to tell the whole schoolhouse. Finally, when Emma suggested that maybe one of these days we could do a real play, like *Hamlet,* Buster burst out laughing. "Emma wants to do a play about a ham!" he cried. "Want to fry up some eggs too?" Pretty soon everyone was calling her Egghead.

But Emma didn't seem to mind being called Egghead. And she knew everyone's lines, not just her own, so if you froze up, she'd prompt you in a whisper. That won Sally and Jill over.

Couple of days later she brought in a book with color pictures of circus animals. Little Ben and his big brother Nathan crowded around her to see the lions and tigers, and in their excitement, they forgot they thought she was a show-off. Finally, Emma's mama sent a basket of biscuits for everyone to share one cold February afternoon. Then even Buster had to admit, "That Egghead ain't so bad."

Two days later, on February 7, 1918, we were in the middle of a long division test when Pa came to school and pulled me out of class. It was my thirteenth birthday and I was awful glad to see him, especially since I hadn't studied. He wouldn't tell me where we were going, 'cept to say it was a big surprise for my birthday. I knew I was finally gonna get "the talk."

But when we got outside, Emma and Mr. Walker were waiting in Pa's car. "We're all going to Tuscaloosa to celebrate our birthdays!" exclaimed Emma. Her birthday was a week after mine, and I guess it was a nice idea, but it meant that— again—I wouldn't get to be alone with my pa.

Emma, Mr. Walker and Pa chattered away like squirrels in an acorn tree. When we passed a sign reading, WELCOME TO TUSCALOOSA, I gave up pouting and started to get excited too.

I had been to Tuscaloosa a couple of times before, but it was usually on some holiday to visit relatives. I wondered if we were gonna see Pa's oldest sister, Ida. Aunt Ida's house was full of tiny, porcelain figurines. I never got through a visit without breaking something.

But instead of turning onto Aunt Ida's road, Pa dropped us off at a theater on Main Street. Pa told us he and Mr. Walker were gonna do some shopping and would pick us up after the show. Then they handed us two tickets and walked away.

Me and Emma gave the usher our tickets. He took one look at Emma and pointed to the stairs. At the top of the stairs was a balcony, looking out over a large theater. We found two plush velvet seats and sat down. A moment later the lights dimmed and the play started.

It wasn't like no play I had ever seen, and I had seen half a dozen between church and school. Huge people walked across the stage. They smiled and their lips moved, but I couldn't hear what they were saying. An organist in the corner played loudly, drowning them out.

Suddenly there was a large train on the stage. It came closer and closer. It was gonna run us over! I scrunched my eyes closed and waited a long time.

Finally, I opened my eyes. There were people and horses on the stage now. The train was gone. "Emma," I whispered, "this is a mighty strange play."

"It isn't a play, Dit," Emma said. "It's a moving picture."

"Oh." I stared in silence at the rest of the film.

When it was over, we stumbled blinking into the bright afternoon sunlight. Pa and Mr. Walker were waiting for us on the sidewalk. They took us to a diner where we stuffed ourselves on hamburgers and pie.

Emma told her daddy the entire story. "And then the bank robbers came and threatened to shoot everyone. And Dit was scared!"

"I was not!" I lied.

"You were too. But so was I. And then a posse came and rode after them and shot them all dead."

Mr. Walker smiled as he picked at his apple pie. "Sounds like you two enjoyed yourselves."

"This was the greatest day ever," Emma gushed.

"Oh, don't say that yet." Pa reached into his jacket and pulled out four more tickets. On the tickets, in small neat letters, was printed: RINGLING BROTHERS CIRCUS.

I was so surprised, I nearly choked on my piece of cherry pie. Pa had to pound on my back till I coughed it up.

All my dreams of going to the circus came rushing back when I handed the bearded lady at the entrance my ticket. I followed Pa, Emma and Mr. Walker into the big white tent. There were wooden benches for us to sit on and three separate rings. I wanted to see everything, but how could I look in three directions at once? We finally picked a bench in the middle and sat down.

In the first ring were the animals. A trainer put his head into a lion's mouth and the crowd roared. Elephants stood on their back legs. Monkeys came out riding bicycles. I had seen pictures of these animals in Emma's books, but the pictures didn't show how they moved or the sounds they made. Seeing them in real life was like having a snowflake melt on your tongue for the first time.

The trapeze artists were in the second ring, men and women dressed in sequined outfits that shone like sunlight on water. Every time they leaped, I had to cover my eyes. But Emma stared. "They're beautiful!" she whispered.

"Are they dead yet?" I asked, peeking out between my fingers.

"They aren't going to fall!" Emma scoffed.

In the third ring was the Wild West show, a mini-rodeo with a cowboy roping a calf, riding a bucking bull and shooting up white men dressed like Indians. The Indians had feather headdresses big as watermelons and as colorful as fall leaves. I could picture them running up and down our mounds, their feathers bobbing in the wind.

I thought my eyes were gonna fall out of my head, I was watching so hard. I didn't even blink. 'Cept once, I looked over at my pa and saw he wasn't watching the circus, but me and Emma with a big, big smile.

37

I OVERHEAR ANOTHER CONVERSATION

MRS. WALKER HAD REALLY COME AROUND to the idea of Emma being in the play. In fact, to hear her talk, you'd think she'd come up with the idea herself. She sent a telegram to a friend in Boston, who mailed her a piece of brightly patterned cloth. The multicolored fabric came "straight from Africa," as Emma reminded me at least once a day. Instead of cutting it up and sewing it, Mrs. Walker showed Emma how to tie and pin the cloth so that it made a dress.

Emma drilled me on my spelling while her mama washed, combed and plaited her hair, finally adding shiny, colorful beads to the ends. Pearl so loved the beads, she begged Mrs. Walker to do the same to her hair. "Your hair won't hold, sweetie," Mrs. Walker said to Pearl, but she did it anyway, covering Pearl's head with tiny, tight braids. That evening Pearl drove our family crazy shaking her head to hear the beads rattle. Every time she did so, a few more beads would pop off and go flying. We spent most of the evening picking colored beads off the floor.

I wanted to look just like the lion tamer in the real circus, so Mama spent hours sewing together bits of leather left over from patching saddles to make me a fringed vest that looked like it had been mauled by a lion. Pa even found an old whip in the barn from when we had horses instead of a car. Ulman loaned me a pair of boots that were only a bit too big, Ollie cut down a thick leather belt to my size and Elman threw in an old hat. When I swaggered into school for the first dress rehearsal, Mrs. Seay smiled and said, "Can I help you, Mr. Lion Tamer?" Even Buster laughed and said, "Roar, roar!"

A few days later me and Emma were helping Mr. Walker sort the mail. Actually, me and Mr. Walker were sorting; Emma was hiding in the back corner, reading her birthday present. Her mama had given her a book of poems by a Robert Snow or Ice or something like that. The front bell rang and Doc Haley came in. Mr. Walker looked up. "Hello, Doc," he said. "You expecting a letter?"

"No. I wanted to speak to you," said Doc Haley.

Mr. Walker stopped sorting.

"A couple of us at the church been a little concerned about you lately," Doc went on.

I ducked behind a sack of mail, hoping the men would forget I was there. Grown-ups always have the most interesting conversations when they forget you're around.

"Why is that?" asked Mr. Walker.

"We don't think your daughter ought to be in that school play."

Emma finally put down her book. Mr. Walker laughed and continued sorting.

"Mr. Walker, we've spent a long time getting where we are today," Doc went on. "And a couple of families are afraid your daughter being in that play is gonna bring on a whole new bunch of problems."

"Well, I thank you for your concern, but there's nothing to be worried about."

"Mr. Walker, this here's Alabama. You might be a big shot up North, but here you're just another Negra. You don't play by the rules, you're risking trouble."

"Mr. Haley, I play by the rules. And if I'm told to take the postmaster's exam every year, I'll take it, even if white men only have to pass it once. But I'm risking trouble every day I show up for work." He struggled with his pant leg, pulling it up. His calf was lined with twisted old scars. Emma winced, even though I'm sure she'd seen her daddy's leg before.

"I received this coming home from my first day of work in Boston. Seems like some white boys didn't like getting their mail from a nigger. But there are some things that are worth fighting for. You'd do well to remember that."

He jerked his pant leg back down. "And if your own self-respect isn't worth that much to you, think of Elbert. I'm not going to tell my own daughter she can't be in a play because of the color of her skin."

Doc Haley shifted his weight from one foot to the other and stared at the ground. "Now, Mr. Walker, I didn't mean to—"

"You want to do something for this town? Next time you see an injustice, take a stand. It's worth the risk."

Doc Haley turned and stomped out.

Mr. Walker cursed up a storm, then remembered we were still there. "Get back to work, you two," he snapped.

We jumped up and started sorting.

38

THE FIGHT IN THE SCHOOL

THE NEXT THURSDAY WAS THE DAY EVERY-thing started to go wrong. I should've realized it. Should have fallen out of bed and stubbed my toe or something. But that's the problem. Those days start like any other.

It was the twenty-first of February—the day of the final dress rehearsal. After school, Mrs. Seay moved her desk aside and set up a little platform for Emma at the front of the room.

"Now turn your attention to the death-defying tightrope walkers, who will dazzle your eyes with their feats of balance." Emma's voice was loud and clear, just like the ringmaster in the real circus.

Pearl and Mary, wrapped in yards of pink tulle, ran out and started walking on a thin wooden plank. Mary immediately fell off.

"Girls!" Mrs. Seay cried. "Slower is better."

"It don't look so good," pouted Mary.

"It looks better than falling off!" I called out. Everyone laughed.

Mrs. Pooley poked her head in the front door. "Mrs. Seay,

I got those new hairpins you wanted." She looked around the classroom. "What the heck is going on?"

"We're having our dress rehearsal," said Earl.

I stepped onto the stage. "Watch as I bravely put my head into the ferocious beast's mouth. I pet his mane and he purrs like a kitten."

Buster crawled over to me, a thick yarn mane wrapped around his head. "Roar! Roar!" he cried. I hit him with the whip. Might have been a bit too hard, 'cause Buster called out, "Hey!" and rubbed his back.

"Sorry," I said, pretending it was an accident.

Emma walked back to the platform, her colorful dress wrapped around her. "And now Raymond the Renegade will perform feats of marksmanship!"

Raymond stepped up front with a lasso. He had spent hours practicing with it in our front yard. He swung it high in the air and knocked over a pile of books. Mrs. Seay scurried over to pick them up.

"What's she doing up there?" asked Mrs. Pooley.

"Who?" I asked.

"The Negra."

"That's Egghead," said Buster.

"Emma," I corrected. I watched her proudly. "Ain't she good?"

I didn't see Mrs. Pooley leave, but I can imagine her hobbling down the street to get Big Foot. If only she had fallen and broken her dang leg. Or if Doc Haley hadn't been out sweeping and hadn't seen Mrs. Pooley and Big Foot come back into the school. Or if Mr. Walker hadn't told Doc to stand up for himself. Or if Emma had just left. Or if I had managed to keep my mouth shut. But wishing you had done things different ain't never changed a thing.

We were just finishing up when it happened. Most of Mrs. Seay's hair had fallen out of its fancy braids and the room was a mess. Bits of costumes and pieces of script were scattered everywhere. Emma stood in the middle of the stage, saying her final lines. "And so I thank you all for coming to our show today. We hope you have . . ." Emma trailed off, staring at the back of the room. She never forgot her lines, so we all turned to look.

Big Foot stood in the doorway. Mrs. Pooley hovered just behind him.

"Mrs. Seay," he said in his slow drawl, "this here's a white school." The click of his boots echoed in the silent room as he approached Mrs. Seay.

"I know that, Sheriff."

"Then what the heck is that nigger girl doing up onstage?" He leaned against a desk, real casual, but the muscles in his neck were tense. Mrs. Pooley stepped inside the school and shut the door. I jumped.

"Emma was the only one who learned the lines," Mrs. Seay said quietly.

Big Foot shook his head and turned to stare at Emma. Her dress, which had seemed so bright and pretty, suddenly looked all wrong. Emma picked at a red stripe on the fabric. Her hand trembled.

"You, girl," Big Foot said, "get down from that platform and go on home."

"But she ain't done with her part yet," said Pearl.

Big Foot glared at my little sister.

"It's the last rehearsal," Pearl explained.

Emma didn't move.

Big Foot took a step closer to Emma. "Girl, I ain't gonna tell you again. Go on home."

But Emma didn't move.

I stepped into the aisle in front of Big Foot. "Leave her alone!" I yelled.

I thought he might hit me, but Big Foot only laughed. "You defending your nigger girl? Ought to have better sense than that, Dit." He pushed me out of the way. I could smell the beer on his breath and see the creases from the iron on his shirt. He walked right up to where Emma was still standing on the stage.

"Big Foot, please," Mrs. Seay said. "The children are just—"

"Be quiet, ma'am. You're the teacher, but I'm the sheriff."

Mrs. Seay was quiet.

Big Foot put his face right up next to Emma and hissed, "Get out of here, nigger!"

Emma blinked and stared at the floor.

Big Foot grabbed her arm and pulled her off the stage. Her dress caught on a desk, causing her to fall. Emma didn't make a sound as she hit the ground, but Pearl began to cry.

The front door squeaked open and Doc Haley stepped inside, standing next to Mrs. Pooley.

Big Foot picked Emma up and threw her over his shoulder like I'd seen my pa do with a sack of potatoes. Her face was strangely blank, like she wasn't even there no more. I wanted her to cry or scream or something. What was Big Foot gonna do to her?

Doc Haley stood in front of the doorway. "Get out of my way," barked Big Foot.

"Put her down," said Doc Haley. "She can walk out on her own."

"I gave her the chance. She didn't move."

"She's too terrified; any fool can see that."

Big Foot dropped her then. Just let go of Emma's feet and she slid right down his back. Her head made a loud *thwack* as it hit the floor. I ran over to her. Blood was pouring out of a gash on her forehead. I pulled off my vest and pressed it against the cut.

Big Foot didn't seem to notice. He walked up to Doc Haley.

"Mrs. Pooley, do something!" cried Mrs. Seay.

"Big Foot," Mrs. Pooley mumbled, grabbing her son's shirt-sleeve. "This is not what I—"

"Hush, Mama."

He shook her off, then leaned over and hissed in Doc's face, just like he had done to Emma, "Get out of here, boy."

"No." His voice trembled, but he held his head up. "Not till you leave these kids alone."

"I said move."

Doc stood so still, I wasn't sure he was even breathing. Then he shook his head.

Big Foot punched him in the jaw.

Doc staggered but remained upright.

Big Foot slugged him again.

Doc fell to the ground this time. Blood flowed from his lip to his chin. He covered his face with his arms. "Get up!" Big Foot screamed.

Doc didn't move. For a minute, I thought he was dead, but then I saw his chest moving up and down. Slowly, he uncovered his face and pushed himself up from the ground like an old man. He stood there, blood running down his face, and even though he was a good four inches shorter than Big Foot, he suddenly looked like the bigger man.

The front door was still open, but Doc didn't even glance at it. Just stood still and looked Big Foot straight in the eye. Outside, the sun was shining, and I didn't understand how that could be when everything was so dark inside.

Big Foot charged Doc Haley then, ran at him liked a crazed bull. They both fell out the open door. We could hear punches being thrown, and then there was the crack of something like a broken bone. Hearing the fight was even worse than seeing it, 'cause we didn't know exactly what was going on.

But with them out of the building, Mrs. Seay seemed to suddenly remember that she was the teacher. "Earl, Raymond, out the window," she ordered. "Go get Dr. Griffith."

My brothers opened the window, jumped out and took off at a run.

I removed the vest from Emma's forehead. It seemed like the bleeding had slowed, but it was hard to tell. There was blood all over my pants and matted in Emma's hair. My lion tamer vest was ruined. Emma's eyes were still blank, and that scared me more than all the blood.

Me, Mrs. Seay and Pearl led Emma out onto the front porch of the school. Doc Haley and Big Foot were still fighting in the middle of the street. Doc was curled up into a ball. Big Foot was pounding him with his fists.

Pa and Earl came running down the street. Pa grabbed Big Foot and pulled him away from Doc Haley. "I'm gonna kill you!" Big Foot snarled. For a minute, I thought he meant my pa.

"I ain't done nothing!" Blood streamed from Doc Haley's face, and his arm was twisted at an odd angle.

Big Foot's clean shirt was now covered in blood. "Just you wait," Big Foot hissed as he shook himself loose from Pa and stormed away.

Mrs. Pooley was very pale as she stumbled out of the schoolhouse. "I—I didn't mean to cause so much trouble," she stammered. No one answered her. She shook her head and hobbled off after her son.

Pa turned to Doc. He was lying in the gravel in the middle of the road, propped up on his one good arm. One eye looked bigger than the other and his lip was so swollen, he couldn't close his mouth. "You all right?" Pa asked.

"I ain't hit him, Mr. Sims," Doc said, "not even once."

"I know," said Pa.

Then Doc Haley collapsed, unmoving, on the ground.

39

DOC HALEY TAKES A STAND

I'D SEEN A PERSON KNOCKED OUT BEFORE—
Ulman was thrown off a horse a couple of summers ago—but
he woke up right away. Doc just moaned a little as Dr. Griffith,
Pa and Raymond carried him back to the Walkers' cabin. Me
and Earl helped Emma home. I expected her mama to start
hollering when she saw us, but I guess someone'd run ahead
to warn her because she just pursed her lips and hurried us
inside.

Pa and Raymond lay Doc Haley down on the couch in the
parlor. Mrs. Walker didn't say nothing, not even when they
got blood on her good sofa.

Dr. Griffith sat Emma down on a chair in the kitchen. He
had to put in five stitches to close the gash in her forehead,
and she didn't make a sound. But when Dr. Griffith finished
sewing and went into the parlor to tend to Doc Haley, Emma
finally started bawling. "Oh, Mama," she sobbed. "I'm not
going to be in the play." Mrs. Walker put her arms around her
and let her cry.

Doc Haley was hurt bad. His left arm was broken; he had
two black eyes, a split lip, a twisted ankle, a couple of bruised

ribs and a lump on his head the size of an old twine baseball. Dr. Griffith set the arm, bandaged the ankle, stitched the lip and put a raw steak over his eyes.

"There's not much else I can do," Dr. Griffith told Mrs. Walker. "Those ribs'll hurt like hell when he wakes up."

"I have a poultice," Mrs. Walker said.

Dr. Griffith nodded. He glanced at me and Emma, then silently went out the door.

That night there was a meeting on the Walkers' front porch. Dr. Griffith and Pa were there, as well as Reverend Cannon from the Negra church and a couple of Mr. Walker's friends. They even let Elbert sit in, but me and Emma were told to stay in the kitchen.

Course as soon as they closed the door, we slid off our chairs and put our ears to the door. Didn't really need to sit that close 'cause Dr. Griffith was practically yelling.

"Absolutely not! He's in no condition to be moved."

"Big Foot find him again, he'll be a whole lot worse," said one of Mr. Walker's friends.

"Elbert," the reverend said quietly. "You have any kin up north?"

"A cousin in Chicago." Elbert sounded scared, and that scared me.

Didn't hear what the reverend said then, because Doc Haley came out of the parlor. He was no longer bloody, but he looked awful, with dark bruises springing up all over his face. "Are they talking about me?" he asked in a whisper, clutching the door frame with his good arm.

I nodded.

Doc took a deep breath, then started limping toward the

front door. Emma jumped up to help him. "Open it," he said to me.

I threw the front door wide open.

Everyone turned to look at Doc Haley, standing in the doorway. "I ain't going nowhere," he said finally.

"But Pa," Elbert started to argue.

"I own the shop free and clear and the field behind it too. It's my land and my home." He looked tired then. Almost lost his balance and had to lean on me and Emma for support. "I ain't going nowhere."

The reverend shook his head. "You're risking your life every moment you stay in Moundville."

Doc Haley looked at Mr. Walker then, and the two men exchanged a glance that was almost a smile. "I thank you kindly, Reverend Cannon, for your concern. But I've made up my mind. And I think it's time for all of you to get on home."

Tired as I was, when I got into bed that night, I couldn't sleep. Finally got up and went downstairs to get some water and found Pa sitting on the front porch with the shotgun. An oil lamp was still burning in the Walkers' cabin, but everything was silent. I slipped into Mama's chair. The squeak of the rocker sounded loud in the night.

Pa jumped. "Oh, it's you."

"Thought I'd sit up with you," I said.

"No."

"But . . ."

Pa shook his head. "Go get some sleep, Raymond."

"Pa, it's me."

Pa rubbed his forehead but said nothing.

"Dit!"

"Go to bed, Dit."

"Would you really shoot Big Foot if he came round to-night?"

"Big Foot's not coming," he snapped.

"Then why're you sitting out here?" I asked.

Pa's face was pinched, as if he had a stomachache. "'Cause if he did come round, he wouldn't be alone."

"What you talking about?"

Pa rocked a couple of times in his chair before answering. "Dit, sometimes a group of people comes up with a stupid idea. An idea so stupid, none of them would be fool enough to act on it alone, but together they . . ."

Pa didn't finish his sentence. I thought of Chip and Buster locking me in jail and knew what he meant. The thought made me shiver, and it wasn't even that cold.

"I can't explain this now," Pa said, rubbing his head again. "Just go to bed."

"But I . . ."

"You talking back to your pa?"

"No, but . . ."

There was a sound in the bushes.

Pa jumped to his feet, clutching the shotgun.

A man was standing in the shadow of the big oak tree in our front yard. It looked like he was carrying a gun.

My hands suddenly felt very cold.

"Who's there?" Pa cried out. He sounded scared.

"It's just me," we heard Dr. Griffith say. "Didn't think you should be sitting up alone." Dr. Griffith stepped into a patch of moonlight, and we could see his face. Pa finally lowered his gun.

"He's not alone; I'm here with him," I called out.

"Dit?" Dr. Griffith sounded surprised, almost angry. "What the heck is he doing out here?"

"He's going to bed," Pa growled.

"But . . ."

"Harry Otis, get back inside the house," Pa hissed, and I knew if I talked back again, there'd be a whipping for sure.

So I went. But I stopped when I got inside the door and looked out the front window. Dr. Griffith was on the porch now. He put a hand on my pa's shoulder and said a few words I couldn't hear. Then he sat down in Mama's rocker, his gun across his lap. Both men sat quietly, looking out into the night.

I went upstairs to bed. But I didn't sleep. Instead, I kept watch out my window too.

40

THE PLAY

THE NEXT AFTERNOON, ME AND EMMA SAT on the top of our mound, just looking at the sky. I was awful tired, but I guess I must have slept some 'cause I remember seeing the starry sky one moment and Raymond shaking me awake for chores the next. On top of the mound, the February wind was cold, but the clouds it brought with it were amazing. I just wanted to stare at them and think about nothing.

"Do you remember the Wild West show at the circus?" Emma asked suddenly.

"Yeah." The one cloud did look kind of like a bronco. I wanted to ask her if she thought so too, but it just seemed like too much trouble.

"Do you think the cowboys killed the Indians that built these mounds?"

"I don't know."

Emma began to cry. I wanted to put my arm around her but wasn't sure if she'd like it. "If I had just left when Big Foot told me to," she said.

I couldn't think of nothing to say.

"I thought I was smarter than all those white kids. That's why I learned those lines."

"You are smarter."

"Shut up, Dit." But she stopped crying, sniffed and wiped her nose on her sleeve. "You going to the play tonight?"

"I don't know," I said.

"Aren't you the ringmaster?"

I shook my head. "I wouldn't do it. Pearl and Raymond dropped out too."

"Aw, Dit," she said softly. "They didn't have to do that. Pearl was so excited about being the ballerina."

"I told Mrs. Seay if you weren't in it, there shouldn't be no play."

Emma smiled, but she still looked sad.

That night I did go to the play, just for a minute. The schoolroom was packed. I guess most everyone in town had heard about the scuffle. Don't know why that made them come. Did they think there was gonna be another fight? Doc Haley was still at the Walkers', and Big Foot was nowhere to be seen. Anyway, Buster stood on the stage as the ringmaster, reading from a script.

"Welcome, ladies and gentlemen, to the most fantastical circus of the cemetery, I mean cent-ury." Big Foot's eagle sat in its cage on a table behind Buster. He pointed awkwardly to it. "Here is the eagle, symbol of my adopted country, the great us-a. I mean U-S-A."

I couldn't watch any more and went out to sit on the front stoop. Pearl was already there.

"Don't you want to go in?" I asked her.

"No."

"Buster's doing a bad job."

Pearl sniffed. "Don't expect me to feel better just 'cause Buster can't read."

I smiled and sat down next to my sister. Sometimes, she was okay. A moment later, Mrs. Seay came out of the schoolhouse and sat down next to us.

"You were right, Dit," she said softly. "We should've canceled the whole thing." The three of us sat quietly in the darkness. Mrs. Seay sniffed a couple of times, like she was trying not to cry.

Finally, Mrs. Seay blew her nose and said, "You know, not everyone in town thinks Big Foot is a good lawman."

"You said he was. In class, when Uncle Wiggens was there." It was a rude thing to say, and I knew it.

"Well"—she took a deep breath—"I've been known to be wrong before."

41

FISH AND BANANAS

PA AND DR. GRIFFITH KEPT WATCH FOR two more nights on our front porch, then they put their guns away. Guess they thought the whole thing was just about ready to blow over. Doc Haley stayed in the Walkers' parlor for another week, till his ankle had healed enough for him to hobble around without help.

Big Foot didn't leave his front porch for that whole week, just sat there and drank beer. The bottles lined up all along the porch. Finally, someone stole the bottles for the deposit money. I had wanted to but hadn't dared.

Elbert quit going to school and started working in the barbershop full time. Doc couldn't cut hair or give shaves with his arm broke, so Elbert took all that over. Me and Emma brought Doc and Elbert biscuits from Mrs. Walker and half a ham from my mama. We shucked some corn too and left it all in a basket behind the barbershop.

I made another trip to Selma with Dr. Griffith the first weekend in March. He didn't mention that night on my front porch, and I didn't say nothing about it either. On that trip, I finally earned the last of my Fourth hunt money. The next morning, I took all my pennies, nickels and quarters to Mrs. Pooley's store and had her change them into two new, crisp dollar bills. I folded them carefully and stuffed them into my pocket. I was gonna carry them with me everywhere till the day of the Fourth hunt finally came.

It was a fine sunny day with no clouds and just a touch of wind. I went by Emma's to see if she'd come fishing with me to celebrate.

"I'm not celebrating you entering the Fourth hunt," Emma said, "'cause I still don't think that's such a good idea. But earning a whole two dollars"—she smiled—"that's really something."

I grinned and hoped my pa would think the same.

"Are you going to ask Elbert to come too?" asked Emma. "Didn't he help you when you were collecting the scrap metal?"

"Yeah." The truth was, I was a bit nervous about getting the two of them together. Elbert had never seemed too fond of Emma.

"Well, I don't mind," said Emma. "If you want, ask him."

So we headed off to the barbershop. I was sure Elbert was gonna say no, but to my surprise, Doc Haley told him to take the afternoon off. So the three of us hitched a ride down the road and ended up at the same fishing hole where me and Pa had run into Emma and Mr. Walker.

Even sat on the same log across the river. I was in the middle, with Elbert on one side and Emma on the other. It was as awkward as it had been all those months before. The fish weren't even biting.

"So, Emma," Elbert said finally, "Dit tells me you like to read."

"Yes, I do," said Emma. "How about you?"

"Naw, not so much," said Elbert.

"Oh," said Emma.

This was not going well.

"Tell him about that book you read," I coaxed Emma. "The one with the map."

"*Treasure Island?*" asked Emma.

"Yeah."

"I don't think Elbert'd be interested."

"Oh, come on, Emma. It was great. It had those pirates, and oh, tell him about the boy who was raised by the apes!"

"That's *Tarzan*," said Emma. "You're mixing them up."

"A boy was raised by apes?" asked Elbert.

"In a secret garden," I explained. "And there was this boy in a chair with wheels and—"

"The ape boy?" asked Elbert.

"No, no, this was a different boy," I said. "And he found a treasure map and convinced this girl, Jane, to go sailing with him."

Emma laughed. "You're messing it up on purpose now!"

Maybe I was.

"Let me get this straight," Elbert said. "You got a book about pirates, ape boys, sailing girls and buried treasure in a secret garden?"

"No, no, no!" Emma laughed.

"Well, shoot, if we'd had books like that in school, maybe I'd like reading!" Elbert exclaimed.

We all laughed then and soon the fish started biting and I shouldn't have worried because it turned out Elbert and Emma got along just fine.

• • •

We walked back to town carrying a whole string of fish. Soon as we reached the edge of town, we saw Uncle Wiggens hobbling by on his wooden leg. He was eating a banana.

"Hi, Uncle Wiggens," I said. "Where'd you get that?"

"Banana train's in town," he told us as he took another bite.

We took off running for the train depot. Bananas arrived in New Orleans by ship. Occasionally, a passenger train would load up a car or two full of bananas and post a man in each car to sell the stalks as the train made its stops.

Sure enough, soon as we reached the depot, we saw the special car, loaded up with green and yellow bananas. The banana man sat on top in a yellow uniform and cap, calling at the top of his lungs, "Bananas! Fresh bananas for sale!"

"How 'bout a free sample?" I yelled to the man.

"Yeah, right, kid," the man called back. "I give you a free taste and pretty soon this whole platform'd be swarming with people begging like monkeys."

This set the three of us off giggling, especially since we'd spent half the afternoon talking about Tarzan and his apes. Besides, it seemed like half the town was there anyway. Dr. Griffith and Mayor Davidson each bought a bunch. Mrs. Pooley bought a whole barrel of green ones for her store. Even Doc Haley wandered over from the barbershop, just to watch all the commotion.

"Oh, please, sir," Elbert cried out as the train started to pull out of the station.

"Maybe just a real ripe one you couldn't sell to anyone else," pleaded Emma.

"Ooo, ooo, ah, eee!" I cried out, jumping around like an animal.

The man finally grinned and tossed down three ripe bananas.

We didn't get bananas too often. Emma peeled hers carefully, trying to make it last. But I gobbled mine down, just as fast as a monkey. Elbert did the same. Doc Haley laughed. "You kids that hungry, come on over to the barbershop and I'll fry you up that fish for dinner."

42

OUT OF THE FRYING PAN

IT HAD BEEN JUST ABOUT THE PERFECT afternoon. Me and Elbert were setting the little table in the corner of the barbershop. Emma was eating the last of her banana as she watched Doc Haley fry up the fish on the tiny stove.

"That's not how my mama cooks fish," Emma said.

"Well, girl," Doc Haley said pleasantly, "you'd better pay attention, then, 'cause once you taste my cooking, you're gonna want to show your mama how it's really done."

Emma laughed. The bell on the front door jingled, and we all turned to see who it was.

Big Foot stepped into the store. His shirt was rumpled, and there was a stain under his right arm. The fading bruises on Doc's face were blue and purple. The frying fish sounded awful loud.

"Elbert," Doc said finally, "go get Big Foot's hair tonic."

Elbert rushed to get the tonic. He returned in a moment and handed the small bottle to his pa, who, in turn, held it out to Big Foot.

But Big Foot didn't take it. Instead, he shook his head and said, "Thought you would have skipped town by now."

"This here's my home, Mr. Big Foot, sir." Doc Haley stared at the ground like he'd done something wrong.

Big Foot plucked the hair tonic bottle from Doc's hand and put it in his pocket. He turned to go.

Doc Haley cleared his throat. "Excuse me, Sheriff?"

Big Foot turned back.

Doc Haley looked him straight in the eye. "Are you gonna pay for that?"

Big Foot didn't move. A muscle in his cheek twitched as he finally put his hand into his pocket and dug out a quarter. He let the coin drop onto the tile floor.

Doc Haley took a step forward to pick it up and Big Foot punched him in the stomach. Doc doubled over in pain and Big Foot hit him again, knocking him to the ground.

I couldn't believe it. This couldn't happen again. What if Big Foot hurt Doc worse this time? Elbert stood frozen and Emma wouldn't meet my gaze. Big Foot kept kicking Doc as he lay on the floor and I knew I had to do something. "You think you're such a big man, beating up your own brother!" I called out.

Big Foot stopped kicking Doc and turned toward me. His scar shone white as ice on his left cheek. "What did you say?" he growled.

I glanced at Emma standing by the stove. Dr. Griffith had taken out the stitches, but if you knew where to look, you could still see the small pink mark on her forehead. "Nothing." I stared at the floor.

Big Foot took a step toward me. Doc Haley struggled to his feet. "Don't you touch him, Big Foot."

"Shut up, nigger."

"He's just a child. If you need someone to hit, hit me."

Big Foot turned back to Doc. "You've been talking."

Elbert flashed me a look that would have just about killed me if I hadn't already felt like I wanted to die.

"I ain't said nothing," said Doc.

Big Foot pulled out the large pistol from his hip and aimed it at Doc. "Then how does he know?"

"I don't know." Doc's face was ashen, but his voice was steady.

"Tell me, nigger, or I'll shoot!"

Emma threw the pan of frying fish into Big Foot's face. He lost his balance, and as he fell, his gun went off. Doc Haley dove behind the barber chair. I grabbed Emma's hand and pulled her under the small table in the corner. Elbert pushed over the shelf and ducked behind it.

"Goddamn it!" Big Foot slapped at his face, frantically rubbing off the hot oil. It left a large red welt on his right cheek.

Doc crouched on the floor behind the barber chair and desperately searched a low drawer.

Big Foot scrambled to his feet and picked up his gun. "Come on out!" he cried.

I didn't know if he was talking to us or Doc Haley or Elbert. I could see Doc still rummaging through the drawer.

Doc finally pulled out a small pistol.

"I said, come on out!" yelled Big Foot. Me and Emma didn't move. Big Foot was between us and the front door.

Doc ducked out from behind the chair and aimed his pistol at Big Foot.

Big Foot stumbled back in surprise and almost tripped on the frying pan on the floor. "So the nigger has a gun," he said tauntingly.

"I'm not gonna let you shoot me."

"I told you I was gonna get you. You should've left when you had the chance."

"I never did nothing to you."

"Just 'cause we had the same daddy don't mean you're my equal," said Big Foot.

"I never said you were my equal."

"Get up off the floor so I can shoot you like a man."

"No."

Big Foot fired his gun, but Doc Haley squirmed out of the way. The bullet bounced off the barber chair and hit a mirror, causing shards of broken glass to rain down on the floor. From under the table, I could see Doc behind the chair, the pistol shaking in his hand. Big Foot approached the barber chair, his boots crunching on the broken glass. He was too close to miss now, and his finger was on the trigger.

Doc aimed for Big Foot's leg, but the sheriff spun the chair around, hitting Doc's arm. Both pistols went off at once. The bullet from Doc's gun hit Big Foot square in the chest. The sheriff gasped and fell to the ground, twitching wildly.

Doc Haley dropped his gun and scrambled to his feet. With his one good arm, he snatched the gun from Big Foot's hand and tossed the weapon into the back room. Big Foot stopped moving, but the red stain in the middle of his dirty shirt kept getting larger. Doc grabbed a towel from the barber chair and pressed it into Big Foot's chest, trying to stop the blood.

"You all right, Pa?" asked Elbert, standing up from behind the overturned shelf.

Doc glanced at the mirror and saw the blood running down the side of his head. He tried to wipe it away with another towel, but his legs collapsed under him and he fell to the floor. Only then did we realize he'd also been shot.

43

CORN BREAD LIKE SAND

DOC HALEY WAS THROWN IN JAIL THAT very afternoon. Dr. Griffith barely had a chance to stitch up his head before Mayor Davidson came to take him away. Me, Elbert and Emma all swore the killing had been self-defense, but Mayor Davidson just shook his head.

"What else you gonna do with a Negra who shoots a white man?" he asked.

"Jail's probably the safest place for you right now," Dr. Griffith said to Doc. "At least till things calm down."

Doc Haley didn't answer, but he went quietly as Mayor Davidson led him off to jail.

That night, I relived the scene in the barbershop over and over in my dreams. Each time, I kept my mouth shut and both Big Foot and Doc Haley got out alive. And each time I awoke, I realized that dreaming ain't worth squat. The only thing I was good at was killing things.

The next morning I went by the jailhouse. Just snuck in the same back door me and Chip had used and walked down the stairs. Doc Haley was in the same cell I had been locked in, sitting on an old dirty cot. He looked like he hadn't slept a wink.

"Hi," I said quietly. "I brought you breakfast." I passed a couple of my mama's biscuits through the prison bars. Doc Haley took them and ate them, but he didn't say a word. I could see the stitches where Dr. Griffith had sewed up the side of his head. I forced myself to look Doc straight in the eyes, but he wouldn't return my gaze.

"I'm sorry, Doc," I said finally. "I never meant for this to happen."

"I know, Dit."

I expected him to be angry or maybe even scared, but he just sounded sad. That made me feel even worse.

"If you hadn't fired, Big Foot would have killed you," I said.

Doc Haley shook his head. "I don't think the jury will see it that way."

We stood there in silence for a long moment. The clock in city hall struck eight.

"I gotta go now," I said finally. "But I'll visit you every day after school."

"No," said Doc firmly. "I don't want you to come here again."

"But . . ."

"Dit, there's just one thing I'm asking of you and it's this." He paused to make sure I was listening, then spoke real slow. "Go home and don't come back."

He lifted his head and looked at me then, and his eyes looked just like a dog who's broke his leg and knows you're gonna put him down.

That afternoon after school, I stopped by the barbershop. Figured it would only get harder the longer I waited. And I had to see Elbert.

Elbert was on his hands and knees, scrubbing at the blood-stains on the floor. Soon as I set foot in the barbershop, he stopped and looked up. "What do you want?"

"Elbert, I . . . I'm really sorry."

"You should be. It's your fault my pa's in jail."

"I didn't mean to . . ."

"But you did," Elbert snapped. "You told the secret I trusted you with."

"I'm sorry." I didn't know what else to say.

"If you had just kept your mouth shut for once, this wouldn't have happened." He was yelling now, but I didn't even flinch. I'd meant well, but he was right.

"I'll tell the judge what really happened and he'll—"

"Don't you know nothing?" yelled Elbert. "Your opinion means squat. All that jury's gonna hear is my daddy shot a white man."

"I'll find a way to make it up to you."

"How?" Elbert scoffed. "What you gonna do?"

He was right. There was nothing I could do. There was nothing else I could say.

"Just get out of here. And don't ever come back!"

I ran. Down Main Street and across the field and through the woods and all the way up the mound to our secret cave. I sat there in the dark with the door closed and cried. Not sure how long I stayed there. After a while, I realized Emma had come in too. She didn't say nothing, just handed me a root beer and we drank in silence.

My nerves were rubbed raw as a peeled carrot by the time Big Foot's funeral rolled around. I had known Big Foot my entire life—how could I not go to his funeral? On the other hand, attending seemed disloyal to Doc Haley and Elbert. But they weren't talking to me, so I went with the rest of my family.

Big Foot looked handsome and peaceful lying in his coffin. He was dressed in his pa's Confederate uniform and a starched white shirt. I stood a long time, looking into his still face. They'd put something on his cheeks, 'cause I couldn't see his scar. Pa stood behind me and didn't say a word.

After Big Foot's body was in the ground, everyone met for a potluck supper in Mrs. Pooley's store. I hung around outside and watched Mayor Davidson turn Big Foot's things over to Mrs. Pooley. There wasn't much—just the deed to the old house, the eagle in her cage, a large ring of keys and a small suitcase. Mrs. Pooley started crying. Mayor Davidson patted her back as she sobbed.

I went inside and ate some chicken I couldn't taste. For once, I wasn't hungry. Even my mama's corn bread tasted like sand.

44

THE TRIAL

DOC HALEY'S TRIAL WAS HELD IN SELMA 'cause Moundville was too small to have its own courthouse. Besides, the district judge said passions ran too high here for a fair trial. So we followed events in the newspaper. Every evening I'd pick up the newspaper from the 7 p.m. train and run home. Pa would pull up a chair close to the kerosene lantern and Mama would settle down with her sewing in her lap. Three or four of us kids would sprawl out on the floor and listen while Pa read the paper aloud.

The paper made it sound like Big Foot just walked into that barbershop, looking for a haircut. Everyone in Moundville knew that wasn't true. It didn't mention that the sheriff had a gun or point out that Big Foot had fired first. I thought me and Emma'd be called to testify, but the paper said we were just children who "couldn't be trusted." Made me madder than a stepped-on bee, but there wasn't nothing I could do.

A couple of newspapermen did come to Moundville to talk to me about the shooting. I answered their questions, then told them they should also speak to Emma, 'cause she was there too. Most just ignored me, but one leaned over and said in a quiet voice, "Boy, no one wants to know what a little colored child saw."

"Why?" I asked loudly. "Her eyes work just as well as mine."

The man turned red. I didn't see him in town no more after that.

As the trial went on, even Mama spent more time ripping stitches out than putting them in. Got so I didn't want to get the paper. But like a fish that can't help snapping at the lure, I always sat with the others on the floor to listen to Pa read us more bad news.

"They can say whatever they want in the paper," Emma reassured me, "but in the end, it's the jury's opinion that matters. We both know it was self-defense, and maybe they'll see that too." I wanted to believe her, but when I repeated her words to Pa, he just shook his head.

Me, Emma and Mr. and Mrs. Walker took the train to Selma to hear the verdict read. We got up early and caught the 7 a.m. train. No one said much, not even Emma.

The courthouse was packed when we arrived. Like the theater where me and Emma had seen the moving picture, whites were on the main floor and the balcony was filled with Negras. I squeezed with Emma and her family onto the balcony. A couple of old Negra women glared at me, and I heard Mr. Walker whisper to them, "He's all right."

Far below us, Doc Haley sat at a small table, Elbert by his side. I waved, but they didn't see me. Doc looked tired, his face pinched, the pale scar from the bullet wound clearly visible.

The jury slowly filed in. They were all white. One man handed an envelope over to the judge.

"Will the defendant rise?" said the judge.

Doc Haley slowly rose to his feet.

"In the state of Alabama, a jury of your peers . . ." said the judge.

Mrs. Walker snorted.

". . . finds you guilty of murder in the first degree."

The room was absolutely silent for a moment, then Doc collapsed into his chair and everyone began to talk at once. The judge pounded his gavel, but no one could hear what he was trying to say. Beside me, Mrs. Walker and Emma began to cry, while Mr. Walker slammed his fist on the balcony railing till I thought it would splinter.

In the courtroom below us, Elbert put an arm around his father. A cold pit formed in my stomach and I felt dizzy. Doc Haley was gonna hang.

45

THE FLU

DOC HALEY WAS TRANSFERRED BACK TO the Moundville jail to wait for his execution. The hanging was scheduled for the end of April, and there wasn't nothing any of us could do.

That Sunday at church, we said a special prayer for Doc. Even Mrs. Pooley kneeled and bowed her head. I tried to sit still and concentrate on the sermon, but Ollie and Ulman couldn't seem to stop coughing, no matter how many times Mama nudged them. Ollie pressed a handkerchief to her lips, but it didn't really muffle the sound. Behind me, Buster and his little brother kept sneezing, one right after the other, like it was some kind of game. When we stood to sing the final hymn, Mama put a hand on her forehead.

"You all right, Mama?" I asked.

"Feeling a little faint," Mama said. She sat back down in the pew as I opened up the hymnal.

Mrs. Weeks was coughing too, and each time she coughed, she missed a note. I thought we were singing "What a Friend We Have in Jesus," but it sure didn't sound like it. I was about to bend down and ask Mama if I'd gotten the song wrong when there was a loud "waaaaa," and the song stopped altogether.

Mrs. Weeks had collapsed forward, her head pressing against the keys of the organ. The instrument continued to bleat out a long, deep note as the preacher hurried over to help her up. Dr. Griffith took her home, but it didn't do no good. By the next morning, she was dead. The flu had come to Moundville.

The flu of 1918 was the worst anyone had ever seen. Oh, we'd had the flu before, of course, but this time the fevers were higher, the body aches stronger, and the coughing brought up blood. People died when their lungs got so clogged, they couldn't take a breath. That was what had happened to old Mrs. Weeks. And this flu spread faster than a piece of hot gossip.

Two days later, a quarter of the children were absent from school. Mrs. Seay tried to carry on, but she looked tired and feverish herself. At recess, Pearl and the other girls skipped rope and chanted:

> *I had a little bird,*
> *Its name was Enza.*
> *I opened the window,*
> *And in-flu-enza.*

As she finished jumping, Pearl had a fit of coughing and my skin went cold.

Mrs. Walker sent a telegram to a friend who was a nurse in Boston. She sent a box of supplies, including a gauze mask Mrs. Walker wore everywhere. "I might look funny," she mumbled through the white bandage, "but I won't get sick."

She went around to all the Negra families in town, offering teas and aspirin from her box.

Dr. Griffith came to our school and hung up a poster from the Health Department telling us ways to stop the spread of the flu. But its warnings—wash your hands, don't share cups and cover your nose when you sneeze—came too late. More than half the school was sick by the first week in April, and Mrs. Seay sent the rest of us home early 'cause she was coughing too.

There was no school for a week after that. The sickest in our family were Pearl, Earl, Raymond and the baby, Lois. They were tucked into cots and couches in the parlor 'cause it was easier to care for them if they were all in one room. Pa, Della, Ollie and Elman weren't quite as sick, so they dozed in their own beds upstairs. For some reason, me, Ulman and Robert hadn't gotten sick at all.

One night, Lois wouldn't stop crying. Mama wiped down the baby's face with a cold rag, but she kept on wailing. Mama's face looked flushed, and I knew she had a fever too. I brought Raymond a glass of milk and cinnamon to help bring down his fever. No one in Moundville had any more aspirin.

Mrs. Walker let herself in without knocking, still wearing her large white mask. She hadn't gotten sick either. "Mrs. Sims, you go lie down," she said firmly.

"But the baby . . ." Mama protested.

"I'll take care of the baby," said Mrs. Walker. "You won't be any good to these children dead."

Mama nodded and went upstairs.

Mrs. Walker picked up Lois and rocked her gently. I was getting pretty tired myself, but as long as Lois was screaming, I knew I wouldn't be able to sleep. I paced quietly, stopping by

Pearl's bed. My sister was a pasty white, her gasps for air louder than a fat man snoring. "Mrs. Walker?" I said, raising my voice to be heard over Lois's cries.

"What, Dit?"

"Pearl don't look so good."

Mrs. Walker put the baby down and came over to Pearl's bedside. She tried not to show it, but I could see her body stiffen as she felt Pearl's forehead. "You'd better go find Dr. Griffith."

I ran. I couldn't imagine life without Pearl. She and Earl were only two years younger than me. Losing one of them would be like losing an arm or a leg. I pushed the thought away and ran faster.

It was after midnight, but it only took a moment for Dr. Griffith to come to the door. "It's Pearl," I said quietly. "You'd best come quick."

Mama and Pa must've been feeling real bad 'cause they didn't even stir when me and Dr. Griffith came in. Mrs. Walker was in the parlor, cradling Pearl in her arms. Lois had fallen into a fitful sleep, but now Pearl was making horrible rasping noises. "Thank goodness!" Mrs. Walker exclaimed when she saw us. "I don't know what to do."

"No one knows what to do," said Dr. Griffith as he put down his black bag.

Mrs. Walker was crying. That scared me more than anything else. Mrs. Walker was the toughest person I knew. "I need to go home and check on my family," she said.

Dr. Griffith nodded. "I'll take over here."

Mrs. Walker handed Pearl over to Dr. Griffith and left the room. Pearl was turning blue. I couldn't take my eyes off of her. "Is she gonna die?" I asked.

199

Dr. Griffith ignored my question. "Dit, I need you to take the Vick's salve from my bag. Melt it in a small pot on the stove. Quickly now, and don't burn it!"

In the kitchen I stirred the salve constantly over a low flame. I always thought Vick's salve was for rubbing on your chest, but Dr. Griffith said he was gonna make Pearl drink it.

"Dit!" Dr. Griffith called from the other room. "I need that salve now."

There were still a few lumps, but I poured the thick liquid into a small cup. It steamed like a witch's brew as I ran into the parlor.

Dr. Griffith grabbed the cup from me and held it to Pearl's lips. She swallowed a sip and began to squirm. She let out a loud gasp, and Dr. Griffith sighed in relief. I sat down on the floor and began to cry.

"It's all right, Dit. She's breathing again."

But I couldn't stop crying. Dr. Griffith sat and rocked Pearl. I cried till I fell asleep on the floor.

46

THE EXAM

THE NEXT MORNING WHEN I WOKE UP, I was still on the floor. Dr. Griffith was gone, but someone had draped a blanket over me. I stood up and looked around the room, counting: Pearl, Earl, Raymond, Lois. Everyone was still breathing.

I wandered into the kitchen. Found Robert standing on a chair, trying to reach the cupboard.

"I'm hungry, Dit," Robert cried.

He was only four. Couldn't expect him to get his breakfast on his own.

"Let me get you a biscuit," I said. I found a couple in the bread box and got out the butter and some jam.

"Eggs, I want eggs," whined Robert.

"Maybe later," I said, placing a plate in front of him. "Eat this now."

Robert dug into the biscuit like he ain't ate in the week. I wondered if anyone had remembered to feed him last night. "Don't be mad, Dit," he said between bites.

"Why'd I be mad?" I asked.

"I broke a glass." Robert pointed to the corner. "Wanted some milk."

"I ain't mad," I said. "Let me get you that milk."

While Robert drank his milk, I swept up the broken glass. Seemed awful quiet in the kitchen with just me and Robert 'stead of Mama and Pa and everybody else.

"Ain't you gonna eat nothing?" Robert asked.

I shook my head. I wasn't hungry.

Mrs. Walker came down the stairs and into the kitchen. I guess she'd come in sometime in the night. I was awful glad to see her.

"How's everyone?" I asked.

"All alive in this house," she said, stirring a pot I hadn't even noticed on the stove.

"And Emma?" She and her daddy had come down with the flu a couple of days before.

"Emma's almost all better. Mr. Walker isn't doing quite as well, but he's on the mend."

I nodded, and my stomach unknotted just a little.

"I'm going to take this broth up to your parents," Mrs. Walker said, pouring the soup into smaller bowls.

"Can I do anything?"

"Maybe tonight you could stop by to read to Emma and Mr. Walker. I'm sure they'd be most grateful for the distraction."

"Sure," I said.

"I'm still hungry, Dit," Robert piped up.

"Come on, then," I said. "Let's go see if those chickens have laid any eggs."

That evening when I came by, Mr. Walker was still in bed, softly snoring. I sat on a chair next to his bed; Emma dozed on a pallet on the floor. She was weak but feeling a lot better. I held her book of poems open on my lap but didn't feel like reading.

"You all right, Dit?" Emma whispered.

"Buster died yesterday," I said softly. "Dr. Griffith told me tonight when he stopped by."

"Oh," said Emma.

I stared out the window. Buster hadn't been too nice to me, but I hadn't wanted him to die.

"I'm sorry, Dit."

"Why should you be sorry?" I snapped. "He was always mean to you."

"Don't say that!" Emma sounded upset. "Mama says it's awful bad luck to speak ill of the dead."

My mama said that too.

Emma thought for a moment. "Buster liked my mama's biscuits. It's not much nice to say about him, but it's something."

It was true. Buster hadn't been all bad. I remembered playing marbles with him when we were small and roasting chestnuts and swimming in the Black Warrior. He'd gotten real quiet when his pa left and real loud when Emma came to town. While we were doing the play, I'd thought maybe he was changing again. Now we'd never know how he would have turned out.

"I ain't never known someone my own age who died," I said finally.

"I did," Emma said. "A girl in Boston."

"What happened?"

"She was playing in the street and got hit by a streetcar."

"Was she a good friend?"

"Not really. But I went to her funeral and played a song on the piano."

"Did it make you feel better?" I asked.

"A little."

If Buster could die, other people I knew could die. Like Doc Haley. Course I'd known he'd been sentenced to death, but I didn't quite believe it, not even after hearing the verdict read. But now, it suddenly seemed possible. And that was just too scary to think about. "It ain't fair," I mumbled.

"No, it's not." Emma reached out from her bed and took my hand. Made me feel a little bit better.

Mrs. Walker came in carrying a tray of food. Emma quickly dropped my hand.

"Time to eat, dear," said Mrs. Walker as she put down the tray and gently shook her husband awake.

Mr. Walker rubbed the sleep out of his eyes. "What time is it?"

"After nine, Sunday evening." Mrs. Walker took a bowl of soup from the tray.

"Sunday!" Mr. Walker exclaimed. "I've got to be in Selma tomorrow for the postal exam."

Mrs. Walker shook her head. "You're in no condition to go anywhere."

"Leah, I've got to take that exam. Without it, there's no hope of getting a transfer."

Mrs. Walker sat down on the bed. "What time is the exam?"

"Eight in the morning."

"It's no use. The last train already left."

Mr. Walker propped himself up on his elbows. "Why didn't you wake me sooner?"

"You've been delirious the past three days!"

"If I don't get that transfer . . ."

"I know what's at stake here," Mrs. Walker snapped. "But I figured I'd rather have my husband alive in Moundville than dead in Boston."

"Don't be so dramatic. I'm not dying."

"But other people are! I've got to wash the bodies for two more funerals tomorrow and . . ." Mrs. Walker covered her face with her hands. "I'm sorry. I'm just so tired, I don't know what to do."

There was a long silence. It got more and more uncomfortable, till finally I said, "I could drive you to Selma."

Mr. and Mrs. Walker turned to look at me.

"Dr. Griffith trusts me to drive into Selma to pick up his supplies," I explained. "I know the way."

Mr. Walker smiled. "You'd do that for me, Dit?"

"Sure."

Mrs. Walker shook her head. "No way. Absolutely not. I will not let a child drive you all the way to Selma in the middle of the night."

"Dit's not a child," Emma snapped. "He's thirteen!"

"And you've done so much for our family," I added. "I'd be glad to help."

In the end, Mrs. Walker gave in. She had to. 'Cause of the flu, there really wasn't anyone else.

47

DRIVING TO SELMA

PA AGREED TO LET US TAKE HIS CAR. MADE
me feel real proud. He wanted to drive Mr. Walker himself,
but Mama wouldn't let him since he still had a fever. It was
decided that Emma would go with me so in case something
happened, at least there'd be three of us. Mrs. Walker wanted
to go too, but she had the two funerals the next day and Mama
still wasn't feeling that well herself.

We tucked Mr. Walker into the backseat of the car and
covered him with blankets. Emma sat in the front, and I was
behind the steering wheel. Mrs. Walker handed us a basket of
food, told us for the thousandth time to be careful, and we
drove off.

Vines hung like thick snakes on the trees alongside the
road. It was the coldest April anyone could remember. An icy
rain fell, coating the leaves and branches so that they glim-
mered in the moonlight. Mrs. Walker had packed us a big thermos of strong coffee. Made me feel real grown-up every time
Emma poured me a dark black cup. Mr. Walker dozed in the
backseat. Every once in a while, a tree branch gave way with

a large crack and fell to the ground. 'Cept for the moon and the car's lights, it was as black as the belly of an eel.

Me and Emma shivered in the front seat. We were wrapped in blankets, but it was so cold, I could see my breath as I drove. Another tree branch fell under the weight of the ice, and me and Emma both jumped. I had to drive at a snail's pace. And the truth was, I'd never driven at night before.

Emma groaned. "I just thought of something."

"What?" I asked.

"If you hadn't offered to drive, Daddy wouldn't have been able to get to the exam."

"And?"

"My family would've had no choice but to stay in Moundville."

"Oh." I hadn't thought of that. Would I ever learn just to keep my dang mouth shut?

We drove in silence for a while longer. Suddenly, there was a loud pop. I thought it was another tree branch till I saw the white smoke billowing out from under the hood.

"What'd you do?" asked Emma.

"Nothing!"

Of course 'cause I was looking at the smoke, I didn't see the ice. Next thing I knew, I was pointing the steering wheel straight and the car was turning, turning till we were sliding sideways down the road. Did exactly what Dr. Griffith told me not to do then—stamped down on those brakes hard as could be.

That did what Dr. Griffith had warned me it would do—set the car off spinning faster than one of baby Robert's tops. Emma screamed and gripped the door. Mr. Walker woke up with a snort, yelling, "Stop the car, stop the car," over and over, like that was gonna help. I started praying, but the only prayer that came to mind was "Jesus, Joseph and General Lee" and I didn't think Emma would like that too much, seeing how Lee was a Southern general, so I just said it in my head. I was pretty sure we were all gonna die, so it didn't much matter what I did anyway.

The car spun around at least twice till we were sliding down the road backwards. Finally I decided to try the brakes again, and I guess we were off the ice because they worked this time. Sort of. We skidded off the road and only ran into a small tree, thanks to my steering while looking backwards over my shoulder. Well, if I'm being real honest, I think I accidentally steered us into the tree, but the important thing was the car was stopped and none of us was dead.

I think Mr. Walker might still have had a touch of fever 'cause he started crying, "Praise the Lord," over and over again, and it was just about as annoying as yelling, "Stop the car." Emma finally told her pa to hush and then I knew he really was sick because he listened to her.

That's when I got scared. We were two children out alone in the woods with a delirious adult and a broken-down car.

"What happened?" said Emma.

"Don't know," I said.

We slid out of the car and I opened the hood. Didn't know what I was looking at for a moment, but then everything Dr. Griffith told me slowly started to come back. I pointed. "So cold, the water must've froze in the radiator. Pressure blew the top right off."

Emma was impressed. I knew she was 'cause she opened

her mouth like a fish but couldn't get nothing out, just nodded and closed her lips again.

"Gotta get to Selma," Mr. Walker moaned from the back of the car.

"So what do we do now?" asked Emma.

I checked the radiator again. It was about dry. "We need to go find some water."

So me and Emma tramped off through the woods. The fog was so thick, it was like stepping through a rain cloud. We stayed close to each other. I carried the cup from the thermos.

"Emma?" I asked.

"Yes?"

"Want me to tell your daddy we couldn't find a stream?"

Emma shook her head. "He wouldn't believe you."

Right then, I think he would've believed me if I'd said I was Abraham Lincoln. But I didn't want to scare Emma. We pushed through some underbrush and stood on the edge of a small creek. The moonlight sparkled on the water. I leaned over to fill the cup.

"Want me to have an accident?" I asked, looking at Emma's reflection in the water.

"What?"

"If I did, we wouldn't get there in time," I said quietly.

"But you'd get in trouble with your pa for wrecking his car."

I shrugged. "I don't care."

"You'd do that for me?" Emma's eyes were wide.

"Yeah." I stood clutching the freezing cup.

Emma smiled. "I don't want you to do that, Dit."

"Do you want to leave Moundville?"

Emma shook her head. "You're the best friend I've ever had." Then she kissed me on the cheek. Before I could move, she dashed up the hill and disappeared into the fog. I touched my cheek and went to follow her.

Once we added the water to the radiator, the car started up just fine. Steam still trickled from the hood, but the engine sounded strong. I had to take it real slow on the icy patches, but there were stretches of dry road that were okay. Mr. Walker went back to sleep. I kept glancing at Emma, but she wouldn't meet my eye.

48

FLOUR AND HOT CHOCOLATE

WE GOT TO SELMA AROUND SIX IN THE morning. The hotel where the exam was being held was right next to the drugstore where Dr. Griffith always bought me lunch. We parked the car out front, then Mr. Walker went into the lobby to register for the test. The fever'd finally broke in the night and he seemed a lot better.

Me and Emma wandered into the steaming kitchen to warm up. We sat on the radiator shivering, still in our jackets and mittens. All the guests I had seen in the hotel were white. All the cooks in the kitchen were colored. One of them gave us a friendly smile and brought us each a mug of hot chocolate.

"Thank you, sir," said Emma to the cook.

He nodded and returned to his post.

For a moment, we sipped our drinks quietly. "Emma?" I asked.

"What?"

"You'll write to me, won't you?" I asked. "When you're back in Boston."

"Maybe Daddy won't pass the test."

I gave her a look. Mr. Walker was as smart as his daughter.

Emma sighed. "Yes, I'll write."

"And visit in the summer?" I pressed.

She shook her head. "Mama wouldn't like me coming down south alone. But you could visit me in Boston."

I'd never been out of Alabama.

"Or maybe we'll move to Virginia," suggested Emma.

"Richmond," I answered confidently.

"Or Connecticut."

"Hartford."

"Or New York."

"New York City?" I asked.

"Albany."

"I knew that," I said with a smile. We sipped our hot chocolates. The cook made the hotel's morning bread, dumping empty flour sacks onto the floor.

"Nothing's gonna change, is it?" I asked. Sounded like there was a frog in my throat.

Emma turned toward me. "Dit, everything's going to change."

I didn't look at her. Just stared at my hot chocolate. It was thick and sweet, made with real chocolate and milk. Just the color of the skin on Emma's cheek. "Why'd you do that?"

"Do what?" she asked.

I touched my cheek.

"Oh." Emma exhaled. "I don't know."

I finished my hot chocolate. The cook came over to take our mugs. "Where you kids from?" he asked.

"Moundville," Emma replied.

"Moundville," the cook repeated when he returned to pounding the rising bread. "Ain't that where that Negra murdered the sheriff?"

"It wasn't murder," I snapped, "it was self-defense."

"Really?" asked the cook. "They didn't put that in the papers."

"We were there," Emma insisted.

The cook shook his head. "You kids," he mumbled to himself. "Active imagination." He emptied more bags of flour into a huge vat. The flour filled the air like a white fog. Like the mist that had surrounded us the night before when Emma gave me my first kiss.

Emma abruptly stood up. "I have an idea."

We spent the next hour loading empty flour sacks into my pa's car. Emma wouldn't tell me why 'cept to say it was important and it had to do with Doc and she would explain later. Right when we finished with the sacks, Mr. Walker came out of the hotel.

"I don't think I missed a question," he said proudly. "They won't have any reason not to promote me now."

That was just what I was afraid of.

49

EMMA'S PLAN

BY THE MIDDLE OF APRIL, EVERYONE IN our family was getting better. We were lucky. Most families in town had lost at least one family member to the flu. Mama said it wasn't luck—it was Mrs. Walker. "Without her . . ." Mama just shook her head and didn't finish the thought.

Doc Haley discovered one good thing about being in jail—without any contact with other people, he didn't get sick. And I was awful glad Doc hadn't died of the flu 'cause Emma had come up with a plan to save his life.

We knew we couldn't just let Doc out of jail. Everyone would know he was gone, there'd be a big search, he'd probably be caught and we'd get in a whole lot of trouble. But if everyone thought Doc was dead, there'd be no need to go off looking for him. And those flour sacks were what gave Emma the idea of exactly how we could fake Doc's death.

But we didn't have much time. The hanging was scheduled for the last Saturday in April, less than two weeks away. Luckily, I knew just who to talk to about getting Doc out of jail.

"What do you want?" asked Chip when I pulled him aside at recess. He'd only been back at school a few days. He looked the same, just a little thinner, but he seemed different. He was quieter. Didn't joke as much. Heck, he'd even apologized when he showed Mary the big red scar across his belly and accidentally made her cry. Maybe it was having his appendix out. Maybe it was Buster's death. In any case, for Doc's sake, I'd risk trusting him one more time.

"Nothing much," I said. "Just need a little favor."

"Ain't you still mad at me?" asked Chip.

"'Cause of that little afternoon in jail?" I laughed. "I got no hard feelings about that." That wasn't quite true, but what's a little white lie if it helped save Doc's life?

"In fact"—I lowered my voice and looked around to see if anyone was listening—"I'd like to borrow the jailhouse key myself."

"Why?" asked Chip. "Does this have anything to do with Doc?"

"I can't tell you," I said, "but if you loan me that key for three hours, I'll give you my baseball glove for keeps."

Chip seemed to think that over. "Don't know if I could take the key again," he said. "My pa'd get awful mad if he found out."

"Since when were you ever scared of getting in trouble?"

Chip grinned.

"Besides," I continued, "I don't need it yet. I'll let you know the day before."

"Your good glove?" Chip asked.

"All yours," I said.

"Okay," Chip said finally. "I could use a little excitement after being stuck in that hospital in Selma. They put me in the children's ward!"

"You can't breathe a word of this to anyone."

"Course not!" Chip replied.

And so we had a deal.

Me and Emma moved on to Dr. Griffith next. Even though I already had the two dollars for the Fourth hunt folded up safe in my pocket, I still drove with Dr. Griffith to Selma. Our monthly trip was a week before the hanging, and this time I asked if Emma could come along. Soon as we were out of town, we told Dr. Griffith about our plan. How we were gonna let Doc out with Chip's key, fake a hanging and bury flour sacks filled with dirt in the coffin instead. He listened quietly but shook his head when we were done.

"No," said Dr. Griffith firmly. "I can't get involved in something like that. And you two shouldn't either."

Emma had expected him to be hard to convince, so she had done some reading and found out about this oath doctors took when they finished their training. I think it was called a "hippopotamus oath." In any case, part of it said, "I will abstain from every voluntary act of mischief and corruption," and if hanging Doc Haley weren't mischief and corruption, I didn't know what was. But when we reminded Dr. Griffith about the oath, he laughed.

"That's just some fancy custom they started in France. I didn't take an oath when I graduated from school."

"Oh," said Emma.

"Still," Dr. Griffith added, "those are good words to live by."

"You gotta help us," I said. "You know Doc Haley ain't done nothing wrong."

"A man's got a right to defend his own life; that's true

enough. But the law's the law. You can't take justice into your own hands."

"We know," said Emma. "But that trial wasn't justice."

Dr. Griffith was silent for a long time.

"Please, Dr. Griffith," I said finally. "Elbert's my friend. We can't just let his father die."

Dr. Griffith drummed his fingers on the steering wheel. "Did you know Mayor Davidson doesn't like blood?"

"No," said Emma.

"Once he even fainted when one of his boys skinned his knee. If you could make it look like Doc tried to slit his wrists before deciding to hang himself, I don't think Mayor Davidson would ask to see the body."

"We could do that," said Emma.

I held my breath.

Finally, Dr. Griffith nodded. "I'll talk to Jim Dang-It about hiding Doc till we can get him out of town. With a change or two, your plan just might work."

Six days before the hanging, me and Emma started digging. We made our cave bigger and wider, shoveling the dirt into a flour sack. When it was full, Emma pulled out a needle and some thread she had borrowed from her mama. I sewed the bag shut. With ten kids, my mama said she didn't have time to be sewing buttons back on every time we ripped a shirt. My stitches were big and a little sloppy, but they held the dirt in.

We dragged the sack onto my wagon and pulled it to the iron dealer's place. The old man looked up from his accounts when we entered.

"We need to use your scale," I said.

"Don't let just anyone," said the old man.

"Give you five cents for your trouble," added Emma.

The man nodded and heaved the bag of dirt onto the scale. Emma handed over the nickel.

I shook a finger at him. "And don't tell us it weighs ten pounds."

The iron dealer laughed, but he read the scale carefully. "Twenty-seven," he said.

If Doc weighed about 160 pounds, that meant we needed five more bags. I had finally found a use for long division.

Three days before the hanging, our hands were full of blisters from digging and our cave was twice the size it was before, but we finally had all the bags filled and hidden behind some bales of hay in our barn. Mr. Fulton brought the coffin to the jailhouse that same day. I thought it was awful rude to put it right outside the cell where Doc could see it. But I guess if you were gonna die, you'd have more important things to worry about than looking at your own coffin.

Two days before the hanging, I went to set some rabbit snares in the broom sage patch. Emma promised to leave them alone this time. Also told Chip we'd need the key Friday night.

That left us with one day just to sit and wait.

50

A CHANGE OF PLANS

THE DAY BEFORE THE HANGING, I TIPPED over the bucket when I was milking the cow. I also pinched my pinkie in the outhouse door, lost all my marbles in a game at recess, got every single problem wrong on my math test and broke my brand-new fountain pen by accidentally sitting on it. But what bothered me most was that I still couldn't decide if we should tell Elbert about our plan. I had tried the night before, but Elbert had turned and walked away. I hadn't followed him. Emma thought it was best not to get his hopes up. I guessed she was right.

So after school I walked past the barbershop and went to check the snares I had set. The first two were empty, and I started to get nervous. If I couldn't catch a rabbit, we wouldn't have no blood and the whole plan might fall apart. But in the third snare I found a large brown swamp rabbit. It stared at me with wide, scared eyes. The rope was pulled tight around its left leg. I picked it up by the scruff of its neck, gentle as a mama cat, and untangled its limb.

"It's all right," I said softly. "Everything's gonna be okay." I hated lying, even if the poor old rabbit couldn't understand a word.

I put the brown rabbit into a large basket I had borrowed from my mama. She used it for picnics, and it had a nice lid you could shut with a latch. Stuffed a couple of carrots in too, so at least the rabbit wouldn't go hungry. Took the basket back to our barn and hid it in Pa's old wheelbarrow, next to the stack of flour sacks filled with dirt. The two kittens we had rescued from the river had gotten sleek and fat on the mice in our barn. One of them slept on top of a flour sack. The other danced around my feet, meowing for a bowl of cream like Emma sometimes brought.

I was too worried to eat much at supper that night, even though we had ham, green beans and biscuits with butter and honey. No one said much. I knew they were all thinking about Doc Haley and the hanging scheduled for ten tomorrow morning.

After supper I went over to Emma's to do my homework. Found her crying at the kitchen table. She'd gotten a 75 on a history test. Her mama'd spent the whole afternoon yelling at her and asking why. Emma wasn't good at lying, but she couldn't tell her mama the truth. We'd spent so much time planning recently, she hadn't had no time to study.

"Glad to know you need to study too," I said. "I thought you were just born knowing everything."

Emma cried harder.

"Shoot, Emma, a 75 is nothing to cry over. It's just a number on a piece of paper."

"What if it doesn't work?" Emma sobbed, and I finally realized she wasn't crying about the history test. I didn't have no answer, so I just held her hand and let her cry for both of us.

I went home soon after that and went to bed early. Me, Robert, Earl and Raymond share a bedroom on the second floor. I sleep next to the window. Little Robert was already asleep, and Earl was busy changing into his pajamas. I climbed into bed without undressing and pulled the blanket over my head. In the dark I picked at the lumpy baseball I had hidden under my pillow till I had unwrapped enough twine to make a loop. I slipped the loop around my wrist and pulled it tight.

Instead of trying to stay up till the grown-ups were in bed, me and Emma were just gonna go to sleep and get up later. Emma had her own alarm clock, given to her by her grandma. If she placed it under her pillow, it was just loud enough for her to hear but muffled so it wouldn't wake her parents. I was planning on tossing the baseball out the window so Emma could wake me by pulling on the twine.

I peeked out from under the covers. Earl was in bed with his eyes closed, but Raymond came into the room and saw me looking around. "You still awake, Dit?" he asked.

"Yeah."

Raymond came over and sat down on the edge of my bed. "I'm sorry about Doc."

"Yeah," I said again, praying Raymond wouldn't notice I was still dressed and had a baseball tied to my arm.

"You're closer to him than any of us," Raymond said.

"Yeah," I repeated. Why did he have to pick tonight to be nice?

"Just wanted to say I was sorry."

"Thanks."

Raymond finally said good night, climbed into his own bed and turned off the kerosene lantern. Soon as the light was off, I forced the baseball out the slightly open window. I could feel the twine unwinding as it fell and heard the soft thump as the ball hit the ground. The twine felt like an iron chain around my wrist.

I didn't think I'd be able to sleep at all, but I guess I did 'cause next thing I knew, someone was jerking at my arm. I sat up. The room was dark and my brothers were breathing nice and steady. I peeked out of the window. Emma was looking up at me, one hand still wrapped around the twine hanging down the side of the house.

I grabbed my baseball mitt and carefully slipped out of bed. I could hear Pa snoring gently in the big bedroom at the end of the hall as I crept down the stairs. The clock on the mantel in the parlor read five minutes after midnight.

First thing we did was head on over to Chip's to get the key. Emma held the basket with the rabbit while I threw pebbles at Chip's window. I could hear the rabbit's claws scratching at the reeds as we waited. Finally, Chip pushed open the window and stuck his head out.

"I don't have it," he whispered.

"What?"

"I don't have the key," Chip repeated a bit louder. "I couldn't get it from my pa. Ever since Doc got arrested, he's been carrying it around with him. Even sleeps with it under his pillow."

"You promised," I said. I couldn't believe Chip was letting me down. Again.

Chip shrugged. "There's nothing I can do."

"Who else has a key?" asked Emma.

"I don't know. Big Foot had one. Maybe Mrs. Pooley's got it now." He glanced back into his dark room. "I gotta go." He pulled his head back in and shut the window.

"What are we supposed to do?" I wailed. "Break into her store?"

I looked at Emma. And we both knew what we had to do.

51

THE KEYS

WE SNUCK DOWN MAIN STREET, HEADING toward Mrs. Pooley's store. The gallows loomed in front of city hall. All week Mr. Fulton had worked on them, singing as he sawed and hammered. Emma stopped in front of the gallows and looked up at the wooden structure.

"Emma," I asked quietly, "freeing Doc is breaking the law, ain't it?"

"Yes."

"Ain't that wrong?"

"I don't know." Emma thought for a moment. "Some people helped slaves escape before the war. They were breaking the law, but I don't think they were wrong."

I stared at Emma. I couldn't imagine her a slave. She was too smart. She was too beautiful. Was it possible that in another time and place, that wouldn't have made a difference?

I leaned over and kissed her on the cheek.

"Don't do that, Dit," she said.

"Why not? You kissed me."

"I shouldn't have."

I didn't think so but said nothing. Even Emma was wrong once in a while.

"We'd better keep moving," Emma said finally.

We reached Mrs. Pooley's front porch. She lived in a couple of rooms above the store. There weren't any lights burning, so I figured we had a chance of pulling this off. Soon as I thought that, Emma brushed past one of the rockers, causing it to squeak. I held my breath till the sound faded into the night.

We tried the front door, a large oak slab with a small window. It was locked. I pulled out my pocketknife and fiddled with the lock. Nothing happened.

"Stand back, Dit," said Emma.

I took a step away from the door. Emma held a large stone.

"Emma, no!"

But she threw the stone anyway. It crashed through the front window. I thought we were caught for sure, but no one came by to see about the noise. Guess the old woman was a heavy sleeper. Either that or she'd had a couple of nightcaps.

I carefully reached through the broken glass and unlocked the door.

Soon as we were inside Mrs. Pooley's store, I lit my candle. It flickered, creating strange shadows as we looked down the aisles. I had been through those aisles a thousand times in the daylight, but at night they seemed as strange as a Chinese market.

"Where do you think the keys are?" asked Emma.

"By the register?" I suggested.

Sure enough, right by the front counter there was a ring of

keys hanging on a nail. Emma reached up and took them down. She spread the silvery keys out in a fan over her fingers.

"Which one is it?" she whispered.

"I don't know."

"We'll have to take them all."

"Think we'll have time to bring 'em back before day-break?"

"I don't—"

The front door opened. A figure stood in the doorway, huge and shining in the starlight. "I saw you go in," growled a deep voice. "Come on out!"

For a minute I thought it was Big Foot, come back from the dead. Me and Emma slowly crept forward. By the light of the candle, we saw Mrs. Pooley in the doorway. "What are you doing?" she asked.

I couldn't think of nothing to say.

Mrs. Pooley tried to snatch the ring of keys from Emma, but she stepped back. "We need the key to let Doc Haley out of jail."

Mrs. Pooley ripped the keys from Emma's hands.

"You have to help us," Emma pleaded.

"Don't you tell me what to do. I'm an old woman. I do as I like." She hung the keys back on their nail, then turned her gaze to us. "Come with me."

52

HOW BIG FOOT
GOT HIS NAME

WE FOLLOWED MRS. POOLEY ROUND THE
side of the store to the wooden staircase that went up to the
rooms where she lived. She led us into her kitchen and put on
a pot of water. There was a large knife on the table, and for a
minute, I thought she was gonna stab us both to death and
cook our bones. But she only used the knife to cut a couple of
slices from a pound cake.

A few minutes later we were sitting around her small table,
each with a cup of tea and a slice of cake. Mrs. Pooley stirred
her tea round and round with a spoon, just like Mama did
when there was something she didn't want to say.

"When Big Foot was just a little boy," Mrs. Pooley said
finally, "his daddy would come in from the fields and take off
his shoes. Little Gabriel, that was his name then, would jump
into his daddy's shoes and shuffle around the house. 'Look at
me, Mama!' he'd say. 'I've got big feets!'" She smiled at the
memory.

I finally noticed how thin Mrs. Pooley was. Instead of wrinkles, the skin was pulled tight across her face. Me and Emma
didn't move as she kept talking.

"But he always was a violent boy. Got in fights at school, tortured stray dogs around town. I knew he was naughty, but I loved him anyway. He was my only child." She paused. "You used to remind me of him, Dit. That's why I asked you to run my errands. But you changed."

She took a deep breath. "I think it's terrible that a nice boy like you runs around with a nigger."

Emma stared at her piece of cake. I couldn't take my eyes off Mrs. Pooley. Her dress was a couple of sizes too big, and she had a sash tied about her waist. Without it holding her together, it seemed her old body might just fall apart.

"Course Gabriel had a nigger for a brother. I always pretended I didn't know—never breathed a word of it to my husband—but I wasn't no fool. I knew my husband liked the Negra women, and Doc Haley was the spitting image of him. Thing is, most people didn't see it 'cause they couldn't get past his color.

"But Doc Haley's wife worked as my maid till the day she died. When she was brushing my hair or sweeping the floor, she often talked about what a kind man her husband was. 'Kind' was not a word I'd ever use to describe my son.

"He only got worse as he got older, drinking and brawling in bars. Then there was that man in Selma. I knew it wasn't no accident." Her voice started to tremble. "If Doc got into a fight with Big Foot, it must have been my boy's fault."

Mrs. Pooley sighed and rubbed the bridge of her nose. "There's been enough killing. If I hadn't told Big Foot that nigger girl was in the play, he wouldn't have started fighting with Doc. I already got one of my husband's sons killed. I won't harm the other."

She shifted uncomfortably in her chair. "Go get me the

sugar bowl, Dit." She pointed to a blue ceramic container on the counter. I got up and brought it to her.

Mrs. Pooley cradled it in her wrinkled hands, then took off the lid and dumped the sugar onto the kitchen table.

I stared at her. She was crazy. Any second now she was gonna pull out a gun or a knife—or maybe the pound cake had been poisoned. Not that any one of us had choked down more than a bite.

It was Emma who noticed the bit of silver metal sticking up out of the mound of sugar. She picked it up and shook off the grains. It was a large, silver key.

"Now get out of here," Mrs. Pooley snapped. "Before I change my mind and tell someone what you're gonna do."

53

FREEING DOC HALEY

I DIDN'T REALLY BELIEVE MRS. POOLEY
had helped us till the key turned in the lock and the prison
door slid open. Doc Haley was sitting on his cot watching us.
We stared at each other. Our candles made big shadows on
the wall. Doc made no move to cross the open threshold.

"Quick," Emma said. "Jim Dang-It's going to hide you until
you can get out of town."

"But . . ." Doc started to protest.

"We'll explain later," Emma whispered. "Go."

Doc nodded and brushed past us, disappearing up the
stairs.

Soon as Doc was gone, me and Emma stripped the sheet
from the cot. It was old, but it had a tough hem. I had to cut
the edges with my pocketknife so we could tear it into long
pieces. We quickly knotted the pieces together, making a thick
rope. We had studied pictures of a hangman's noose in a book
at Emma's house and practiced with an old sheet in our cave,
so I thought it would be easy. But our hands shook at every
noise and the minutes stretched out like an old sweater as we
struggled to form the makeshift rope into the right shape.

Finally, it was done. The noose lay on the floor of the cell, still as an albino snake.

Next, I took the rabbit from the basket. It quivered in fear, its dark eyes huge in the candlelight. "Do you have to kill it?" Emma asked.

"Dr. Griffith said we needed blood," I reminded her. "The rabbit was your idea."

She nodded and looked away.

With a snap, I broke the rabbit's neck. It twitched for a moment, then hung limp as an old hat, warm in my hands. Quickly I began to skin it. When I was through, I put the hide aside and took the bloody rabbit meat and rubbed it all over the white noose.

Finally, Emma dipped the sheets in the outhouse bucket. That was real disgusting, but Emma had read that sometimes people peed on themselves when they were hung, and we wanted to make things as realistic as possible.

The noose was a dripping, stinking mess by the time I boosted Emma onto my shoulders. Emma pulled away bits of plaster from the old ceiling till she found a beam. She looped the filthy sheet over it and tied the noose tight. We both hung from the rope, making sure it could hold our weight.

Next, we dragged the cot over so it was under the noose—as if Doc had used it to boost himself to the ceiling. Emma suggested we tip it on its side, as if Doc had kicked it over once he decided to hang himself. Finally, we wiped some blood onto an old, rusty nail, threw the nail on the floor and stood back to look at our work.

"I'd believe he killed himself," said Emma.

"Me too." But I hoped it would fool the people who mattered.

The coffin was waiting in the hall. Me and Emma dragged it into the small room next to the jail cell that was used for a morgue. We struggled to lift it onto the flat table. It wasn't really heavy, just awkward 'cause of its size. Then we ran back to my pa's barn. The bags were too heavy for us to carry, but Emma could pull one in my wagon and I could push two in Pa's wheelbarrow. We thought we could move them all in just two trips.

The first trip went fine 'cept for a raccoon that scuttled across Main Street and scared us half to death. We were almost back to the jail with our second load, and I was just beginning to think we might pull this off, when Uncle Wiggens wandered into the street.

"Who there?" he called out, his words slurred.

Emma ducked behind a tree, but I didn't move fast enough. "Is that you, Dit?"

I nodded. Something was strange about him.

"What you doing out so late at night?" he asked.

"Nothing." I figured out what was strange. "Where's your leg?" I asked. His leg ended at the knee and he was hopping along on one leg and his cane.

"Left it at home," said Uncle Wiggens. "Always do when I'm sleepwalking. My daughter warned me about drinking a whole bottle of whiskey in one sitting. But I was never one to let a woman tell me what to do."

"Yeah. Me neither."

"Well," said Uncle Wiggens, "I'd best get on home before I wake up."

"Yeah."

"Being out without my leg and all."

"That would be embarrassing."

"Sure would. Sure would." Uncle Wiggens mumbled to himself as he wandered off. "General Lee always said, if you ain't got all your supplies, don't ride into battle. Course he meant bullets, but he wouldn't have liked us going off without our legs neither. Course most of us have our legs buttoned on, but . . ."

When he was finally gone, Emma stepped out from behind the tree. "You could have helped me," I said, heart pounding.

"I thought you did pretty well on your own." She giggled, and for a moment, I forgot what we were doing and giggled too.

54

A NIGHT IN JAIL

ONE BY ONE, WE LUGGED THE BAGS DOWN the stairs and lifted them into the open coffin. I got the rabbit skin from the other room and threw it in the coffin as well. Then Emma put in a hammer and a handful of nails we had stolen from my pa's toolshed and closed the lid.

"Do you think it'll work?" Emma asked.

"Course it will." But even I could hear the uncertainty in my voice.

We made our way up the stairs and out of city hall. "What time is it?" Emma wondered.

I looked up at the stars. "About three, I think."

"I better get home."

"Yeah," I said. I handed her the basket with the dead rabbit and reminded her to throw it to our dogs on the way home. I could see the silver key clutched in her left hand. She played with it absently, sliding it between one finger after another.

"Sure you don't want me to stay with you?" she asked.

"Emma." I sighed. "If someone finds me here, I can make up a lie and they might believe me. But if you're here too, we don't have a chance."

She nodded. We'd been over this a million times. But the truth was, I didn't want her to leave. We stood next to each other in the starlight, and I felt her rest her head on my shoulder. I put an arm around her waist. She didn't pull away. We stood like that for a long time.

"Dit?" Emma said softly.

"Yes?"

"Whatever happens, we did the best we could."

I nodded.

She kissed my cheek. I turned to see her face, but she wriggled away and hurried down Main Street.

I went back inside the jail and lay down on the floor in the room with the coffin. It was cold, lying on the hard stone floor. I could hear little claws clattering over the old stones—the rats Chip and Buster had promised would eat my bones. Poor Buster was dead now.

Right now, Emma was taking the key back to Mrs. Pooley. We had promised to leave it under the mat to her back door. But what if someone saw Emma slipping into Mrs. Pooley's yard? Or if Mrs. Pooley changed her mind and told on us? All I could do was sit and wait.

Dr. Griffith was coming first thing in the morning to get Doc Haley ready for the execution. It was really the job of the sheriff, but we didn't have one no more, and no one wanted to hire another. 'Cept for Jim Dang-It, Dr. Griffith was the only grown-up who knew about our plan.

And even though Dr. Griffith had agreed to help us, I couldn't help worrying as I lay on the floor under the table, beneath the coffin filled with dirt. The darkness was thick as pea soup. It pressed on me. My stub of a candle had long since burned out. I began to imagine I was Doc Haley, going to be hung in the morning. A cold panic crept up my throat. What if Dr. Griffith didn't show up? I forced the thought away.

I must have fallen asleep 'cause suddenly there was sunlight streaming in through the small window near the ceiling. I heard voices and jumped to my feet.

Dr. Griffith was supposed to get the key from Mayor Davidson and come alone. He would "discover" the body, then I would just happen to come along on a morning walk and help him cut Doc Haley down. Least that was the story we were gonna tell everyone. By the time anyone else arrived, the "body" would be safely in the coffin, closed and nailed shut, so that no one would have to see the horrible sight. So why did I hear voices? Something had gone wrong. I climbed onto the table next to the coffin and peeked out the tiny window.

Mayor Davidson was standing with Dr. Griffith at the top of the stairs that led down to the jail. Dr. Griffith was real pale. "You really don't have to come down with me," I heard him say. "I can get Doc ready alone."

"Nonsense," Mayor Davidson replied. "I'm up, excited and looking forward to the hanging. I don't mind coming down to give you a hand." He moved toward the stairs. Dr. Griffith put a hand out to block him.

"Larry," Dr. Griffith said firmly. "I shouldn't tell you this, but . . ."

"What?"

"Doc Haley don't like you too much."

Mayor Davidson laughed. "I don't like him neither."

"He's a little unbalanced, what with the hanging today and all. Yesterday, I promised him I'd come get him ready alone."

"A promise to a murderer don't mean nothing."

"I know. I just want to go down first to warn him that you're coming. We've got to put on the cuffs and the ankle chains so he can walk up to the hanging. That could be difficult if he's agitated. And if you show up unexpected, he's going to get agitated."

"All right," Mayor Davidson snapped. "You go down and put the chains on, then come up and get me. Don't want no trouble. Though I don't know when you became so soft-hearted."

"Thank you, Larry."

"Five minutes," Mayor Davidson said. He took a large silver key out of his pocket and handed it to Dr. Griffith. "Then I'm coming down."

Dr. Griffith hurried down the stairs.

55

WHERE'S MY PA?

I MET DR. GRIFFITH AT THE BOTTOM OF the stairs. He was staring at the empty cell. "You did a good job," he said. "If I didn't know better, I'd say he'd really hung himself." He paused and sniffed the air. "The urine was a nice touch."

"Emma's idea," I said.

Dr. Griffith turned and went back up the stairs. I ran back to my perch on the table to listen.

"Doc's dead," Dr. Griffith panted, as if he had run up the stairs two at a time.

"What?" Mayor Davidson turned white.

"Looks like he slit his wrists with an old nail, and when that didn't work, he stripped the sheet from the bed and hung himself."

"Oh my God!" Rivulets of sweat began to stream down Mayor Davidson's fleshy face.

"Is there blood?"

Dr. Griffith nodded. "Lots."

"Oh." Mayor Davidson looked like he was gonna be sick.

"Would you go get Mrs. Walker?" asked Dr. Griffith. "I need someone to help me cut Doc down and put him in the coffin."

"I can do it," said Mayor Davidson, clearly hoping Dr. Griffith would say no.

Dr. Griffith shook his head. "It's a messy job. You'll ruin your suit. There's no need for that. Best get Mrs. Walker. She's a nurse and used to this kind of thing."

Mayor Davidson quickly agreed and ran off.

A minute later, Dr. Griffith joined me in the room with the coffin. I took out the rabbit skin. Some of the blood was still wet, and I helped Dr. Griffith rub it all over his hands and clothes. Finally, we threw the rabbit skin into the coffin, took out the nails and hammer, and Dr. Griffith started to nail the coffin shut.

He was just putting in the last nail when Mrs. Walker, Emma and Mayor Davidson came running. They saw the bloody noose and the open cell and gasped. Mayor Davidson bent over, put his hands on his knees and began to gag.

"How'd you get the body down?" asked Mrs. Walker. "Thought you needed my help."

"Dit came by early to say goodbye to Doc Haley. He helped me."

Mrs. Walker took a deep breath. "Has anybody told Elbert?" she asked.

"No," said Dr. Griffith.

"I'll go." Mrs. Walker glanced at the cell once more, then turned and left the room.

Soon as she was gone, a voice cried out from the stairwell. "Why I keep seeing these people running back and forth? I

239

thought the hanging wasn't scheduled till ten." Uncle Wiggens hobbled down the steps and caught a glimpse of the cell. "I guess someone decided to have the fun a little early."

"It was suicide," said Dr. Griffith grimly.

Uncle Wiggens saw me then and broke into a big grin. He hadn't shaved in a couple of days and gray bristles were popping up all over his face. "Dit!" he cried. "You'll never believe it. I had the funniest dream about you last night."

Oh, no.

"I fell asleep and dreamt that I was walking around town without my leg."

"Without your leg?" asked Mayor Davidson.

"Yes," said Uncle Wiggens, "in my dreams I never have my peg leg, though I never have my whole leg neither. I just sort of hop around. Wonder why that is? Think I could at least dream about having both legs again. Anyway, I dreamt I ran into Dit, and guess what he was doing?"

"What?" asked Mayor Davidson.

"He was walking around in the dark pushing a—"

At that moment Elbert burst into the room. "Is it true? Is it true?" He glanced in the cell and fell to his knees. Mrs. Walker hurried down the stairs, finally catching up with him. She put a hand on his shoulder.

"Where is he? Where's my pa?" Elbert wailed.

"We put him in the coffin," said Dr. Griffith.

Elbert scrambled to his feet. "I want to see him."

"He's in no condition to be seen, Elbert," Dr. Griffith said in the kind, quiet voice he used with patients. "Hanging does terrible things to a man's body."

"I don't care. I want to see him."

"We've already put the nails in the coffin," I said, cursing myself for not telling him.

"Yes," Dr. Griffith added. "I really don't think it's a good idea."

"What are you fools talking about?" Mrs. Walker cried. "If the boy wants to see his daddy's body, let him see it!"

Dr. Griffith slowly began to pull out the nails, one by one. I thought desperately. What were we gonna do? I looked at Emma. She shook her head. Then I had an idea.

"Wait a second, Elbert," I said. Dr. Griffith stopped pulling out the nails. "Why you think your pa killed himself?"

"I don't know," said Elbert, his face a stone mask.

"'Cause he didn't want the whole town to see him dead, hanging at the end of a rope. He didn't want to die publicly. If you open up his coffin right here letting everybody see, you're disrespecting his last wishes."

Elbert thought for a moment. "Dit's got a point. You all turn around and face the other way. I'll open the coffin myself. I'm family. I got a right to see."

Mayor Davidson looked slightly disappointed but also slightly relieved. Dr. Griffith handed Elbert the hammer and we all turned around. I held my breath, praying he would catch on. We should have written him a note or something.

It seemed like it took forever for Elbert to pry up the nails, but it was probably only a couple of minutes. Finally, I heard the last one tinkle to the ground and heard the squeak of the lid as it was lifted up.

"Where's my pa?" Elbert asked.

I spun around and slammed the lid shut.

"Where's my pa?" Elbert repeated.

Emma started crying, loud as a baby with colic.

Dr. Griffith shook his head. "This often happens when the body is so badly mutilated. It's why I didn't want him to look."

Elbert was pale as a corpse himself. "Where's my pa?"

"Your daddy's moved on to a better place," said Mrs. Walker kindly. She moved over to embrace him.

"He was a suicide," said Uncle Wiggens. "Don't they go to hell?"

Mrs. Walker shot Uncle Wiggens a look.

"It's a shame he had to endure seeing the body," Dr. Griffith added.

Emma wailed even louder. Elbert just looked confused. "But where is—" I kicked him in the shins. He gave me a funny look, and then everything clicked into place. "Ohhhhhhh," he said loudly. "He's dead."

"Yes," Dr. Griffith said. Elbert began to cry big, fake sobs. I started to laugh and had to hide it as a hiccup. Pretty soon Mrs. Walker was crying too, and Dr. Griffith wiped a few tears of relief from his eyes. Even Uncle Wiggens joined in.

Only Mayor Davidson stood by, staring at us like we were a bunch of fools. "We need someone to identify the body for the death certificate," said Dr. Griffith finally.

"I can do that," Elbert gasped between fake sobs. "He's all messed up, but he sure is my pa."

56

GOODBYE, DOC HALEY

DR. GRIFFITH RAN HOME TO GET HIS PAPERS. Me, Elbert and Dr. Griffith put our names on the death certificate, then Mayor Davidson signed it, making it official. Doc Haley was dead.

We had the funeral two hours later. Just about the entire town showed up. My family was there, of course, and Dr. Griffith, the Walkers and all the folks from the Negra church. Even Mr. Fulton came, wiping his eyes like he forgot he was the one who built the gallows. Only Mrs. Pooley and Uncle Wiggens stayed away, rocking and smoking on her front porch.

Reverend Cannon kept the service short. The women cried a little, then the coffin was buried outside the churchyard in the plot reserved for murderers, fallen women and suicides.

Afterwards, me and Emma walked Elbert back to the barbershop. On the way, we passed Uncle Wiggens standing in front of Mrs. Pooley's front door. "Somebody done broke your window," we heard him call out.

Me and Emma held our breaths, but Mrs. Pooley only shrugged. "Nothing was missing. Must have been the wind."

Finally, we reached the barbershop. "So where is he?" Elbert asked.

I smiled. "I heard Jim Dang-It say he was real sorry he couldn't make it to the funeral."

"Why don't you go pay him a visit?" added Emma.

Elbert grinned.

At home, I stripped off my clothes and fell into bed. Just as I put my head down on the pillow, Raymond came in and shook my shoulder. "Why'd I find a bunch of old twine outside your window?"

"Don't know what you're talking about," I murmured.

"You didn't come home last night."

I looked up. "Raymond, you can't tell anyone. It's real, real important."

"Then you gotta tell me the whole story."

Raymond's eyes got wider and wider as I told him what we had done, but he didn't say a word. Even did my chores for me that day so I could get some rest. Guess my older brother had loved Doc Haley too.

Chip cornered me the next day after church. He knew something was going on, but he couldn't prove it, least not without admitting he'd been stealing his pa's keys. I gave him my baseball glove to buy his silence. We agreed to say he'd won it from me in a game of marbles.

Me and Emma went to say goodbye to Doc Haley Sunday afternoon. We found him in Jim Dang-It's cabin, sitting by the fireplace with Elbert, drinking a cup of coffee. "Guess I was wrong," Doc Haley said.

"About what?" I asked.

Doc Haley smiled. "'Bout you and Emma being friends."

They invited us in, and there were hugs and cocoa and lots

of mushy stuff like that. I pulled Elbert aside at one point and told him I was sorry I hadn't told him about the plan.

"Dit," Elbert said with a laugh. "You saved him. You can stop apologizing."

Doc Haley left that very night. Jim Dang-It gave him an old dugout canoe so he could paddle up the Black Warrior. When he got to Birmingham, he planned to ditch the canoe and buy a train ticket. Elbert had cleared out their savings, and Doc had just enough. The train would take him all the way up north to his cousin in Chicago. Me and Emma gave Doc our leftover hardtack from the soldiers so he wouldn't starve even if he didn't stop to fish or hunt. Around midnight we said our good-byes and Doc Haley paddled off into the darkness. I had the sinking feeling that nothing would ever be as it was before.

57

GOODBYE, ELBERT

I WAS RIGHT. IT WAS ONLY A COUPLE OF days after Doc Haley left that Elbert asked me to come by the barbershop. The shop was nearly empty when I arrived 'cept for a pair of scissors and a couple of bottles of hair tonic packed in a box.

"I've decided to leave Moundville," Elbert said. "There are too many memories here. I'm gonna make a fresh start up north." He paused. "Least that's what I'm telling people."

I nodded. Elbert had acted as the town barber ever since his father was arrested, but everyone could tell his heart wasn't in it. His haircuts were uneven, and his shaves just about always included a nicked chin.

"I asked your pa to sell the barbershop for me and send the money on after he finds a buyer."

"Don't you want to stay and sell it yourself?"

Elbert shook his head. "Mr. Walker loaned me enough money for a ticket. I don't want to wait any longer."

"When are you leaving?"

"Tomorrow."

"Oh," I said. "That soon."

"Yeah," Elbert said. "I'm all packed and ready to go."

"Oh," I said again. "Anything I can do for you?"

"No," said Elbert. "Well, yes. How about going fishing?"

It was my last time fishing with Elbert on the Black Warrior, and we hardly caught a thing. We said even less, but somehow, sitting together in the afternoon sun, listening to the birds, I knew we were finally back to being friends.

Me and Emma met Elbert at the station early the next morning. She had packed a big basket of sandwiches for him so he would have something to eat on the train. Elbert stood on the platform, clutching the one small suitcase that contained all his possessions. His face was pinched. "I don't have enough," he burst out when he saw us.

"What?" I asked.

"They raised the ticket price. I'm a dollar-ninety short." A whistle blew as the train started to pull into the station. "I can't stay in this town a minute longer," said Elbert. "I just can't." His back was bowed like an old man's. "I guess I'll have to get off when my money runs out and hitchhike the rest of the way." He'd shaved off his new beard, and his naked chin made him look like he wasn't old enough to cross the street by himself, much less hitchhike to Chicago.

I knew what I had to do, but I didn't want to do it. I forced my hand into my pocket and pulled out my two dollar bills.

"I can't take that," exclaimed Elbert. "That's your Fourth hunt money."

"No, it ain't," I lied.

"The hunt's in just a couple of months," Elbert said. "You been saving all year for it."

"It ain't my hunt money," I insisted. But we all knew that it was.

The whistle sounded again and the conductor called, "All aboard!" I pressed the money into Elbert's hand. It was a man's hand, callused from hard work, covered with little cuts from when the scissors had slipped. He whispered, "Thank you," straightened up his back, and I knew he was gonna be okay. He took the basket from Emma, waved to us both and climbed onto the train.

The engine pulled slowly out of the station. Emma started tapping her toes like she was dancing and I could tell she was about to burst with pride over what I had done, but I didn't want to hear it. Elbert stuck his head out the window and for a moment, he looked like my old fishing partner again. "I'll pay you back when I get the money from the barbershop!" he called out.

"Thanks," I replied, but I knew the money would come too late. Me and Emma waved as the train picked up speed, waved till it had disappeared down the track. I had known Elbert my entire life. I didn't think I would ever see him again.

Life finally returned to something like normal after Elbert left. We went to school, played ball. At first it was strange seeing Chip with my glove, but pretty soon, I almost forgot it had ever been mine. The first time Emma hit the ball in an actual game, she was so surprised, she dropped the bat and forgot to run. Pearl had to give her a push to get her moving. It should've been an easy out, but somehow Emma made it safely to first. She jumped up and down like she'd conquered the world.

But things weren't normal, though if you had asked me, I wouldn't have been able to tell you what was wrong. Of course,

Doc Haley and Elbert were gone and Buster and Big Foot were dead, but it was more than that. Things were shook up, like leaves falling in the spring and flowers blooming in the winter.

Even skipping stones at the river was different. Emma kept asking me about the Fourth hunt. "You did the right thing giving Elbert your money," she said. "And you're good at lots of things besides killing things."

"I know," I said.

"So why are you so upset you can't enter?"

I threw another stone. "It was the only way."

"The only way to what?"

"You can't understand."

"Why not?" demanded Emma.

"Your mama and daddy hang on your every word. There are ten of us."

"Oh." She got real quiet then and didn't say nothing else. So maybe she did understand. Maybe that was why she worked so hard in school. Maybe she knew all the things I didn't know how to say about making your parents proud, 'cause she worried about them too.

58

THE LETTER

ON THE LAST DAY OF SCHOOL, THE OTHER students quickly packed up their belongings and ran out. I took my time and made my way over to Mrs. Seay's desk. She sure had changed since she'd first arrived in Moundville. Wore a regular work dress most of the time now. Her hair was pulled back in a simple bun. But even without the fancy clothes, she looked just as pretty as before. "Mrs. Seay?"

She looked up. "Yes, Dit?"

"I have something I need to tell you."

"What is it?" She tugged at the collar of her dress.

I swallowed hard. "I was the one who broke your window. Last summer, before school started. I'm real sorry." I couldn't look at her.

"Thank you, Dit." She paused. "I accept your apology."

I nodded, still staring at the planks on the floor.

"But I always knew it was you."

I looked up. "How?"

Mrs. Seay laughed. "There isn't anyone else in Moundville who's got your arm."

"I'd like to pay for it, but . . ."

"You can make it up to me by helping in my garden next fall," Mrs. Seay said firmly. "Right now, I want you to go home and enjoy your summer."

I ran all the way from the schoolhouse to the mounds, feeling lighter than I had since Big Foot's death. Me and Emma were meeting in our cave. It was a lot bigger now after digging out all that dirt for Doc's coffin. We were gonna make it even better this summer—line the floor with stones and maybe build some three-legged stools so we had some real furniture. But for now, all I wanted was a cool soda and a dip in the river. Maybe, if they were biting, we'd have fish for supper.

I ducked into the cave and grabbed a soda. Emma was already there, clutching a piece of paper.

"What's that?" I asked, taking a sip of my soda.

"A letter," Emma said.

"What's it say?" I asked.

"My dad passed the test."

"What test?"

She looked at me. I started to choke.

"We're going back to Boston," Emma said.

"Oh."

"We leave in three weeks. The day of the Fourth hunt."

The cola burned running down my throat.

"They've already hired a new postmaster. He's got twin boys your age."

"Great." My stomach felt like it had been kicked by an old mule.

"Dit, I—"

"I don't want to talk about it."

"I want to tell you—"

"Shut up!" I ran out of the cave and into the forest. Didn't stop till my legs were aching. Finally leaned against a tree and threw up. When I was finished, I walked on till I found a little stream. I rinsed out my mouth and sat down under a pine tree.

I didn't know where I was.

Maybe that wasn't quite true. I could've figured it out if I'd gotten up and looked around. But I just didn't care no more. I wanted to sit on that bed of pine needles forever.

I sat there all afternoon and evening. Seemed like if I didn't move, nothing would change, and Emma would stay in Mound-ville. I knew that didn't make no sense, but still I didn't move as the sun went down and the stars came out. Sat till I heard a voice in the moonlight.

"Dit, is that you?" Jim Dang-It stepped over the small stream.

"How'd you find me?"

Jim snorted. "Left a trail a mile wide."

I didn't say nothing.

"Your mama's worried herself sick. Get up and get your dang self home."

Slowly, I stood up. My stomach ached 'cause I hadn't eaten anything, and my legs stung from tiny cuts I got running through the underbrush. Jim clutched my arm so tight it hurt, and we started walking home.

After a while Jim's grip on my arm softened. "You know, Dit," he said in a quiet voice, "when my wife died, I was real angry. Angry at the old doctor who wouldn't come 'cause I didn't have no money. Angry at God for taking her away."

Jim paused to make sure I was listening.

"But after a while, I thought of something worse than losing my wife."

"What?" I asked.

"If I'd never met her at all."

We walked the rest of the way in silence. Mama was pacing back and forth on the front porch when we arrived home. Soon as she saw us, she ran down the front steps and threw her arms around me.

"I was so worried, Dit!" Mama cried. "Don't you ever run off like that again!"

And that was when I finally started to cry.

59

THE TALK

THE NEXT MORNING I WOKE UP EARLY AND went outside to chop some wood. My thoughts were still in a muddle, and there ain't nothing like chopping wood to clear your head. I'd been chopping for a good half an hour when Pa came out of the house and walked over to where I was working.

"Dit," said Pa. "I need to talk to you."

"I'm sorry for running off," I said. There was a rhythm to the chopping. If I concentrated real hard, maybe I wouldn't have to think about nothing else.

Pa waved a hand in the air. "Shoot, I ain't upset about that. Your mama worries too much. I knew you were okay."

I kept chopping. "Then what'd you want to talk about?"

Pa was silent for a moment. "I know what you and Emma did," he said finally.

I let my ax fall to the ground. "You do?"

"Dr. Griffith told me," said Pa.

"Oh." I sat down on a stump. "I'm sorry."

"Sorry?" asked Pa.

"Are you real mad?" I asked. Despite all the growing I'd

been doing, Pa was still taller and stronger than me. I wondered if he'd make me cut my own switch for a whipping.

Pa shook his head. "Dit, I'm proud of you."

I stared up at my pa. He was smiling, and in the sunlight, his hair was exactly the same color as mine. "It took a lot of courage to do what you did," he said. "And brains too."

"The brains was mainly Emma," I said.

Pa laughed. "I ain't too good at putting my thoughts into words, Dit. But I wanted to give you something." He pressed some crumpled papers into my hands. I carefully unfolded them. They were two dollar bills.

"Is this so I can enter the Fourth hunt?" I asked.

"You can do whatever you want with it," said Pa.

We stood there in silence for a moment.

"Are you ever gonna give me the talk?" I asked.

"The talk?" Pa asked, then laughed. "Oh, that talk."

"Well, are you?"

Pa shook his head. "The part about girls, it's just too embarrassing. Ask Raymond. But the part about being a man, you don't need that. That you already know."

He put his hand on my shoulder and I felt like a million bucks.

Late that afternoon, I stood on the banks of the Black Warrior. There wasn't no more wood to chop, but throwing stones was almost as good. I skipped them across the water, watching them bounce six, seven, eight times. After a while, I got a prickly feeling on the back of my neck. I looked up.

Emma stood at the edge of the forest.

I nodded at her and went back to throwing stones.

Emma picked up a couple of stones and started throwing

herself. The sun went down some more, and I watched her stones skip across the pink water.

"My pa gave me money to enter the Fourth hunt," I said finally.

"Oh," she said. She opened her mouth like she was gonna argue with me, then closed it. Her shoulders dropped, but she smiled as she said, "Sorry I won't be here to see you win it."

I knew how much she hated the whole idea of the Fourth hunt. Also knew that she finally understood what it meant to me. And now, suddenly, I wasn't sure I was even gonna enter.

"Sorry I ran off yesterday," I said.

"It's okay."

"Do we have to talk about you leaving?" I asked.

"No," said Emma. "Not if you don't want to."

We skipped some more stones.

"You know, I wouldn't have told on you," Emma said finally.

"What?"

"About the window. And the buzzard. Even if you hadn't helped me. I was just bluffing."

"I know." I knew that, and lots of other things. But I couldn't say them. I just took her hand and held it in my own, my fingers next to hers. I couldn't stop staring at them. We stood in silence for a long, long time.

60

THE POSTCARD

FOR THE NEXT THREE WEEKS EMMA HELPED me with my chores so we could spend every waking moment together. When the cows were milked and the garden weeded, we went hiking in the woods and fished on the Black Warrior. We played baseball and drank root beer on Mrs. Pooley's front porch and talked about Emma's books. Me and Emma skipped stones, tossed balls of yarn for the kittens and borrowed Pa's car for a joyride. Only thing we didn't do was talk about her leaving.

The afternoon of July 3, Reverend Cannon organized a goodbye picnic for the Walkers. I went, of course. There were rows of tables set up outside the wooden church and enough food for everyone in Selma. Most of the guests were colored, though my whole family stopped by. Dr. Griffith and Mrs. Seay did too. Even Jim Dang-It showed up, said goodbye to Emma and left without saying a word to anyone else.

Don't remember much about that afternoon. I was trying so hard not to think about what was happening the next day, I didn't even notice what I ate or who I talked to. Emma was busy saying goodbye to everyone else and didn't have much time for me. And so before I knew it, just about everyone had gone home and Mrs. Walker was packing a basket of leftovers to take on the train.

I was just about ready to head on home myself when Emma raced up to me and grabbed my arm. "I got something to show you, Dit."

"What?"

"Oh, no. Not here." Emma shook her head. "Race you to the top of our mound."

So we ran through the forest and up to the top of our mound. It was so easy for Emma now, she didn't even have to look where she was going. Didn't have to think about avoiding the pricker bushes 'cause she knew where they all were, and if a new one had grown up overnight, well, it didn't matter 'cause she had calluses on her hands. She still wore a dress and fancy shoes, but both were patched now and she didn't seem to care. Emma scrambled up the hill ahead of me, and a gust of wind blew a red ribbon from her hair. I stopped to pick it up.

When I finally reached the top, Emma was laughing. "I beat you! I finally beat you."

"Yeah, you sure did."

Emma put her hands on her hips. "Did you let me win?"

"No. Why would I do that?"

Emma smiled.

"You lost this," I said, holding out the ribbon.

"You keep it," said Emma. "I got a million more."

The sun was just beginning to set and had turned everything golden, like a film of oil floating on the water. I put the ribbon in my pocket and asked, "What did you want to show me anyway?"

Emma pulled a small card out of the pocket of her dress and handed it to me.

I looked carefully at the card. On one side was a picture of a tall building. Below it, in printed letters, was the word *Chicago*. I turned the card over. It was addressed to Dit Sims and Emma Walker of Moundville, Alabama. There was a small note next to the address:

> *Both arrived safe.*
> *Thanks again.*

I looked up at Emma. She was smiling. "We did it. They're free."

"I guess they are." I looked down at the card in my hand. Never knew you could feel happy and sad at the same time, but I did, like someone was pulling my heart in two different directions. Maybe that's why I finally found the words to ask, "Emma, why do you have to leave?"

"Dit, I . . ." She shook her head.

"If only I hadn't given your daddy a ride to Selma . . ."

"We would've never found the flour sacks," Emma finished. "And without the sacks we might not have come up with the plan."

"And Doc would've died."

Emma nodded. "It was worth it, Dit."

"But you're my best friend."

"I know. And you're mine."

I handed the card back to her. "You keep it. So you can remember what we did together."

"Don't need a card to remember that." But she took the

postcard, folded it carefully and stuck it back in her dress pocket.

"I'll miss you," I said.

"I'll miss you too," Emma replied.

The sun was almost down now and the fireflies were out, twinkling on and off like tiny floating stars.

"Can I kiss you goodbye?" I asked.

Emma nodded.

So I did. Right on the lips and everything. I probably should say it was gross or something. But it was actually kind of nice.

Then we joined hands and walked down our mound together, one last time.

61

GOODBYE, EMMA

ME AND EMMA STOOD SILENTLY ON THE tracks early the next morning, waiting for the train. The Walkers had all their belongings packed in a few neat, leather trunks. Emma clutched her own small suitcase. Pearl, Earl, Raymond and the rest of our family waited nearby.

It was gonna be a hot July day, but I felt cold. The train whistle made me shiver. When the eagle on the top of the locomotive flew into the station, for the first time ever I didn't feel a thrill. I wanted to shoot it down out of the morning air.

The train lumbered to a stop and people began pouring out. "Bye, Dit," Emma said.

I swallowed hard. "Bye, Emma."

There wasn't time to say nothing else. Her parents bundled her onto the train. Emma turned to wave goodbye, then ducked into the car. A moment later the train pulled off.

"There's the new postmaster," said Pearl, pointing.

A white family stood on the platform. They had three children, a girl who was almost eleven, just like Pearl, and two boys, both thirteen. One of the boys carried a baseball glove.

"Hi, I'm Billy," the boy said brightly. "That's Tommy."

"We're twins," said the other boy.

"But I'm older," said Billy.

"Only by ten minutes." They both had dark hair and light eyes, and if Billy hadn't been carrying a glove, I wouldn't have been able to tell them apart.

Mama made me carry their trunk home in my wagon. The twins chattered like chipmunks the whole way. I didn't say much, and they didn't seem to notice.

"Do you have your own glove?" Billy asked. "I do. See." He held it up.

"I have one too," said Tommy, "but mine's in the trunk."

"Well, do you?" asked Billy.

I just shook my head.

Soon as I could, I snuck off, leaving Billy and Tommy behind. In front of Mrs. Pooley's store was a group of men, registering for the Fourth hunt. Mrs. Pooley carefully wrote down their names and took their money. I stood off to the side and watched them, but I didn't join in. Didn't even feel an urge to take the two dollars out of my pocket.

Instead, I went to the top of our mound and lit a small campfire. I carefully fed it bits of kindling. A train whistle sounded in the distance. I looked up.

Far off, a train was twisting along its track through the forest.

I pulled my flip-it out of my pocket and touched the carefully carved wood. A bird twittered in the branches of a nearby tree, a sparrow sitting on a low branch.

I put a rock into the flip-it and fired. The bird fell to the ground, dead. Gently, I scooped it up and put it down on a large flat rock. Then I tossed my flip-it into the fire.

The fire began to smoke. I picked up an old blanket and began to shake it over the fire, creating great billows of smoke. Probably wasn't doing it right, but I hoped she could see them from the train. Smoke signals telling her how much I would miss her.

I sat on the mound all day till the fire had burned down and I didn't have no more wood. Finally, as the sun was about to set, I saw Mrs. Pooley struggling up the hill, carrying the eagle in its cage.

"I couldn't come till the hunt was over," said Mrs. Pooley. She put the bird down and walked over to me. "Two dollars, we agreed on." She held out her skinny hand.

I carefully smoothed the wrinkles out of the two dollar bills and laid them gently on her palm.

She looked at me suspiciously. "You didn't steal this money, now, did you?"

"No."

"All right, then. Don't know why you want this old bird, but it's yours." She turned and hobbled back down the hill.

I looked at the eagle in the cage. She looked sad, worn down. I approached the cage carefully and unlocked the door. It swung open with a small squeak.

The eagle was surprised. I could tell she was thinking, This has never happened before, not in all the years I've been trapped in this cage. She pushed herself into the bars at the far end of the cage and cowered there.

I picked up the small dead sparrow and put it on the ground, just outside the cage door. "Come on, baby," I said softly. "I killed one last bird, just for you."

The eagle smelled the bird and hopped forward. She poked

her beak out and snatched the sparrow back inside, eating it in two large gulps.

"Come out," I coaxed her. "You're free. Fly away."

The eagle looked at me and cocked her head. At that moment, I would have sworn that she understood. She hopped out of the cage.

I felt the smile on my face, mixing with the tears.

The eagle hopped around once or twice, stretching her wings. Then all at once she jumped into the air. A wind picked up and sent her soaring, far into the rosy evening air, off into the sunset.

ACKNOWLEDGMENTS

I WISH TO THANK THE FOLLOWING PEOPLE for their help with this project. First, a big thank-you to my wonderful agent, Kathy Green, and my talented editor, Stacey Barney, for making the process of completing my first book such an enjoyable experience.

Thank you also to the many people who read this story in all its different stages: Matt McNevin, Neil Conway, Kate Revelle, Sonja Levine, Roseann Mauroni, Ruth Williams and my other friends at Tuesdays at Two; Debbie Gaydos, Kristie Kehoe, John Douglass and my test "kid" readers, Karen and Claire Adler and Ciara Flosnik.

An extra-special thanks to my grandfather, Harry Otis Sims, for writing down his memories of his childhood in Moundville, Alabama. His recollections inspired this story. Thank you also to my grandmother, Maurine Sims, for typing those handwritten pages and to my aunts and uncle, Judy Reed, Joanmarie and H. O. Sims for copying those pages and giving them to all of the grandchildren.

Finally, I want to thank my family: my parents, Tom and Marlene Walker, my sister, Erika Knott, my daughter, Charlotte, and especially my husband, Adam Levine. Without their love and support this book would not have been possible.